A REFLECTION OF RACHEL

By the same author

ANCHORS WHARF
(*Rupert Hart-Davis*)

PINEAPPLE PALACE
(*Rupert Hart-Davis*)

A SERAPH IN A BOX
(*Rupert Hart-Davis*)

LEOPARDS ON THE LOIRE
(*Gollancz*)

A TIME TO DANCE
(*Collins*)

MUSICAL INSTRUMENTS
(*Oliver* & *Boyd*)

A REFLECTION OF RACHEL

ROBINA BECKLES WILLSON

ILLUSTRATED BY
BARBARA BROWN

MACMILLAN
LONDON MELBOURNE TORONTO
1967

Published by
MACMILLAN & CO LTD
Little Essex Street London WC2
and also at Bombay Calcutta and Madras
Macmillan South Africa (Publishers) Pty Ltd Johannesburg
The Macmillan Company of Australia Pty Ltd Melbourne
The Macmillan Company of Canada Ltd Toronto

PRINTED IN GREAT BRITAIN

For Janet, with Love

CHAPTER ONE

EVEN Rachel could not lighten the gloom. Although it was cold and wet, she wished that she were out of doors, instead of cooped up in a small flat with her brother and sister. She leaned against the window, and for once, her plant on the sill, reared from the stone of an avocado pear, did not give its customary pleasure. She stroked a firm, pointed green leaf from the cluster at the top, and admired the sturdy red-green stem, seventeen inches the last time she measured it.

Behind her, Tatiana was darning her ballet shoes, complaining as she did so:

'We'll never get out of this horrible box. Things'll never be the same again.'

'How can they be, for a widow with three children?' Matthias demanded sharply. 'Use your head.'

'I do,' Tatiana answered crossly. 'You don't like it either.'

'Who would, after what we had when Daddy was here. But it's no good bleating. . . !'

'I'm not!' Tatiana pricked her finger, and sucked it furiously.

'Don't try and blame me for that,' Matthias said.

Rachel turned round to them. 'I'm sure we'll find something better in time. It's not easy in London. And at least some things are the same. You can still dance, Tatiana, and your music, Matthias. . . .'

'Nothing could stop me dancing,' Tatiana announced.

'Except a broken leg,' Matthias put in. And he winked surreptitiously at Rachel, so that she was for a moment cheered and said:

'Mummy ought to be in at any minute. Perhaps she's found something this time.'

'She's tried hundreds of agents,' Tatiana exaggerated miserably. 'So why this time?'

'Stop moaning,' Matthias ordered his younger sister. 'She *is* here.'

Mrs David came in, and the three children bustled round her, making tea, and arguing over scorched crumpets.

After they had eaten, Matthias and Tatiana embarked upon homework, and Mrs David took the opportunity to draw Rachel into the kitchen.

'No luck?' Rachel asked her.

'Not exactly. The point is, you realise, that London prices for flats are just about sky high. We have little option but to leave the London area, unless I accept a rather extraordinary job that's been offered to me.'

'What job?' Rachel asked eagerly. 'Is it a nice one?'

'Hard to say.' Her mother smiled ruefully. 'I can't honestly say that I regret one hour of my married life, but it would have been *so* sensible to have finished my course and qualified. Marrying so young was very gay then, but I could have done much better for you all now if I could earn a really good living.'

'You couldn't do better,' Rachel protested. 'We like you as you are. If you'd have spent years and years training, you'd be old now!'

Her mother laughed. 'Hardly. But I could have taken up a more lucrative job to help support us all.'

'All right. I've got the message. We all promise to do a proper training. I'll be a qualified nurse by the time I'm twenty-one, pass all my exams and have gold medals dangling down my starched apron. Will that do?'

'Beautifully. And if someone can push anything into Tatiana's head beyond arabesques and pirouettes that'll be a relief too. Just in case she suddenly shoots up to six feet, or breaks three toes.'

'Don't worry so much. She'll go to one of these schools where they do their lessons before ballet classes. She's going to get a scholarship. It's all been worked out with her beloved Miss Julian. And I bet she will. Now what is this job?'

'A sort of housekeeper's job.'

'Oh,' Rachel said flatly. 'Would you like that?'

'I don't really know. But it would solve a lot of problems.'

'How? Would they pay you a vast salary?'

A*

'No, but it includes accommodation for all of us. That's why it's worth considering.'

'For all of us? How peculiar. They must want a house-keeper pretty badly. Where is it? The Hebrides?'

'No, the London area. It's at Aynescombe Green. You see, it's from your grandfather's cousin, Luke David.'

'Who's he? I've never heard of him.'

'I've never met him myself. When we were married, he sent us a rather odd letter, and I've heard nothing further from him until today.'

'Yes,' Rachel prompted, as her mother frowned in the pre-occupied way which had become such a habit that two sharp lines cut into her forehead above her nose, and were never smoothed away, even when all three of them reduced her to laughing weakness by fooling and teasing.

'He wrote and offered us all a home with him on certain conditions.'

'What? That you act as housekeeper?'

'More or less. I think that he might be rather a difficult old man, but he does say it's a big house, and I do think there'd be a lot of room. We might be better off in the long run, and, if we lived rent free, I would be able to do a lot more for you. Pay for holidays and things like that.'

'If he gave you them! Mummy, wouldn't it be a come-down after being your own boss, even in this titchy little flat? And this place can't be much fun for you after the lovely flat we had before. What does his letter say exactly?'

'I'll read it to you. I'd like to hear your reactions.

' "Dear Cousin Anna,
            It has only recently been brought to my attention by my solicitor that your husband died in one of the aircrashes which so disfigure the travelling conditions of this speed intoxicated century." '

4

'What does he mean by that?'

'I gather he doesn't much care for our times. I won't read it all, but the invitation comes now:

' "I understand that in spite of the measure of success he enjoyed, your late husband left you in severely straitened circumstances. Now this house is a large one, and I should be willing for you and your children to make a home in part of it. Notwithstanding, I should wish to keep my own rooms strictly private, as has been my custom for many years. I should expect to maintain this seclusion my confining myself to the ground floor.

' "In view of the increased difficulty in obtaining the service of reliable and discreet servants, it has occurred to me that you could make yourself useful within this establishment. My own housekeeper, Miss Drube, who has been with me for more than forty years, will continue to work for me, but she complains of finding this large house too much for her as she becomes older: whereas I have not the slightest intention of leaving my home, where my parents and grandparents were content to pass their days." '

'Does he think you're going to clean the whole place then, while his old housekeeper leans on a broom?' Rachel demanded. 'How big is it?'

'I don't know, but the bigger it is, the more room for us all. We've never had enough room here. Matthias' room is no more than a cupboard.'

'And you've had to sleep here in the living-room.'

'I don't mind that,' her mother said quickly. 'We've been reasonably happy and comfortable here, but that may have been because we knew it was the end of the lease, and we'd have to find somewhere else, preferably bigger, fairly soon. I think I ought to go and see this house, at least.'

'We ought, you mean. I'm coming too. I won't tell the others if you don't want me too, but I'm not letting you go alone. This Cousin Luke might eat you! Where is Aynescombe Green? Could we do it in one day?'

'Oh yes, easily. It's only about an hour and a half from here, I should think.'

'Then write back and say that we'll call on him in the seclusion of his ground-floor apartment. Or, of course, in one of the other suites if he prefers!'

'Rachel, what would I do without you? All right, we'll go and see him.'

'*And* his stately home, or mansion, whatever it is. I can easily get a day off school next week. We've finished exams, for the moment.'

'Then I'll write to him tonight. After all, we're not committing ourselves to anything yet.'

Mrs David stared down at the thin black writing, written with a dip pen. This might prove to be an opportunity for them all. It was up to her to make it work. But the sentences she had not yet read to Rachel ran coldly through her mind. It wasn't the warmest of welcomes, and she shivered in spite of the oil heater.

'I am not devoted to children. Indeed, it would be difficult to be fond of the twentieth-century child, for whom so much is done, provoking so little gratitude. Yet I trust that I know my duty even to the more obscure branches of my family, and while you bear my surname, which I assume that you still do, we are connected. Thus I open my house to you and your children.

'I should warn you that I have the strongest objection to noise. I do not approve of television.'

Mrs David broke off. They had not afforded to rent television this year, and the children had visited friends for favourite programmes. But he did sound a bit of a killjoy. Perhaps he just wrote in that stiff way.

'He may be just an old man who is set in his ways,' she told Rachel, while trying to convince herself. 'It would be silly not to go and *see* him. I'll answer this letter at once, not tonight. It'll probably turn out to be quite impossible, and he just made this offer out of a sort of feeling of pity. And really couldn't stand us there.'

'We'll just have to do what you're always telling us to do: "Wait and see",' said Rachel.

Mrs David smiled at her, but as she took out notepaper, she could not keep back the thought: 'I wonder if he counts music as noise?'

CHAPTER TWO

'But I couldn't leave London,' Tatiana stated positively.

'Well, we might have to,' her mother remarked mildly.

'But I couldn't possibly! I couldn't leave Miss Julian. She wants me to try for a scholarship this summer.'

'The white hope of British ballet,' Matthias said, buttering toast with deliberation. 'There are other ballet teachers, you know.'

'Not like Miss Julian. Anyhow, you wouldn't want to leave London either.'

'No, I wouldn't,' Matthias admitted. 'Just when we've got some decent equipment at school. But it's no good getting worked up at this stage.'

'It certainly isn't,' Rachel agreed firmly. 'So you just hold on until we've been to see Aynescombe Green. There may be a chance there. We don't know yet.'

'I think we'll know when we've seen Cousin Luke and the house.' Mrs David was pouring out coffee and milk. 'We'll be able to tell you a lot more this evening.'

'How far out is it?' Matthias asked.

'Just over half an hour from Waterloo. According to the A.B.C. Map, Old Bridge Street is not a long walk from Aynescombe Green station. It would be just possible for you all to stay at your present schools if we did settle there, or give it a try, anyhow. That is part of the attraction, because it's not an easy time to move, with exams on the horizon for you two.'

'I'd much rather travel in than change schools now. Lots of girls do,' Rachel said. 'They do homework on the train. It would only be a train to Waterloo, and a bus or a tube, after all!'

'We'll see. It may not be at all suitable,' Mrs David said cautiously.

'Or he may be a wicked ogre,' Matthias improvised, 'and terrify you so much that you'd never dare go there again.'

'He can't be that bad,' Rachel said peaceably. 'He's made the offer. Nobody asked him.'

'Perhaps he has some dark reason of his own,' Matthias went on, in a sepulchral voice, hoping to scare Tatiana, who was staring at him, forgetting to eat her cereal.

'Don't be ridiculous,' his mother told him, though she smiled. 'I suspect it's purely practical. He wants help to keep the house in decent order; doesn't want it all shut up, and his old maid can't, or won't cope any longer.'

'It would be marvellous to have dozens of rooms,' Matthias said. 'We could really spread ourselves.'

'It won't be that big.'

'You don't know. Ogres usually live in castles, don't they, Tatiana? And we could get the piano out of storage. All my friends who have pianos are sick of the sight of me, and . . .'

'Perhaps they think you're a *noisy* ogre,' Tatiana interrupted triumphantly, and returned to her cereal with vigorous satisfaction, having scored some sort of point.

Rachel did not feel very hungry. She was half dreading the trip, and half looking forward to it, just in case it did produce a solution to one of their problems. She turned to her mother.

'If we had the piano back, you could start to play again. You must have missed it too.'

'I think we all have, in spite of Matthias' records.' Mrs

David was resolutely cheerful. 'More coffee, anyone, or I'll finish it off?'

Rachel ate stolidly, chewing hard against a maddening, unexpected threat of tears, trying not to remember the countless times she had lain in bed and heard her mother accompanying her father as he learned new parts in operas, or as they played and sang together for pleasure. Perhaps it would be easier to start a new life in a new place now that nothing could be taken for granted any more. Even if it was in somebody else's house.

*　　　*　　　*

'Don't you know anything else about Cousin Luke, or whatever he is? You must know something,' Rachel coaxed her mother as they sat in the train from Waterloo.

'Not a great deal, honestly. He wasn't very interested in music and opera; never came to hear your father at Sadler's Wells, even when he had big parts and very good notices.'

'But Daddy must have known him when he was younger.'

'Hardly at all. Old Luke quarrelled with your grandfather, and cut himself off from that part of the family when he lost his wife.'

'She died?'

Mrs David looked confused and Rachel pounced. 'Come on, don't be mean. You *do* know something.'

'Wheedler. The truth is, I don't remember the story properly, and I don't want to tell you a whole lot of old gossip, when we're going to visit him. Or have you pass it on to the other two, particularly Tatiana, to get all upside down.'

'Mummy, don't dodge the issue. What do you know? What happened to his wife? He didn't murder her, presumably?'

'Of course not. That sounds like Matthias teasing Tatiana.'

'It's me, teasing you. Come on, tell.'

'I believe his wife left him. Ran away. And that's all. Literally all. I can't check the story. And neither can you. You have to be a meek and demure audience at this interview, speaking when or if you're spoken to, don't forget!'

'All right, I won't. But I'm not sure I believe that's all.'

'It is. You see, it all happened before I came into the family. The two old men just weren't in touch when your grandfather was still alive, and so we weren't either.'

'This is our station, so I'll let you off,' Rachel said, relenting, as she wanted to concentrate on looking at Aynescombe Green.

The little station had two platforms covered by wooden roofs, painted in cream with cut-out edges, supported by green iron pillars. No one sat on the green benches, and they strolled out of the empty station, giving up their tickets at the doorway, to a small side street. Mrs David consulted the map.

'We turn left up this street on to the Green. Old Bridge Street is at the bottom of the Green, to the right.'

'And Bridge House is there?'

'I think so.'

The Green appeared a somewhat neglected large patch of grass. Old trees rose from newly dug earth, and broken stick fences lay stacked on the ground, as if a gallant attempt was being made to tidy it up for the spring and summer. But this early March day it appeared bare and muddled, surrounded by an odd mixture of tall, ornamented Victorian houses, shops and small factories or works.

'Of course,' Mrs David said brightly as they turned into

Old Bridge Street, 'it will look much better in the summer when those trees and shrubs are out.'

The road was not a wide one and they did not speak as they walked along because the traffic was noisy.

Rachel in any case did not know what to say. She noticed with dismay the forlornly unkempt properties they were passing. A series of empty shops were boarded up. Their old sun-blind supports tipped forward, splitting their beams, their blind chains broken and hanging, swinging thick with dusty rust. One upper window board was smashed in, and a tattered cream blind hung over the gap in strips. The shops were close to the road and dirty. One window was so engrimed that in parts it was completely opaque. Through the centre a dim light came from the back.

A torn flapping poster advertised a 'DISC NITE. Admission free for opening night with THE OBJECTS and THE TWEETS. Girls 2/-. Boys 3/- following nites.'

'I wonder why girls get in for less?' Rachel asked, pointing out the poster.

Her mother smiled absent-mindedly and glanced through the smashed windows of a cottage into the downstairs room, where the ceiling was collapsing.

'Does he really live in a place like this?' Rachel wondered as they passed a black corrugated-iron fence, full of holes where nails had been lost, rusting and frayed at the edges, browning and mottled. Barbed wire and a rickety fence completed that set of properties and they looked with some relief down a small side street they now crossed, with rows of neat brick cottages, each having tall slatted shutters at the upper windows.

'Perhaps this is the respectable end!' Mrs David said. 'There are some new flats coming up over this set of shops. But no big houses yet.'

On their left a long wall enclosed a factory or works of

some kind, but, as the road bent round, the wall ended with a lane. Then there was a row of two-storey houses, built right on to the pavement.

A tall house set back from the road came next, and, without being told, Rachel knew that it was Cousin Luke's house.

'That's it,' she said. 'I'm sure it is.'

They crossed the road, and walked alongside a thick brick wall, over six feet high, to the wooden gate, painted black. It was Bridge House. Rachel looked up, stepping back to the edge of the pavement.

'What a tall house!' she exclaimed.

The windows of Bridge House were long ones divided into eight panes, one on each side of the house on the ground floor, then a wide window on the second floor. To the right of the house an extra wing had been added on two floors.

'We're early,' said Mrs David, checking with her watch. 'Let's go and have a look at the back as well.'

'Yes, and the river.'

Beyond the house was a narrow path, called Bridge Passage. The old wall, curved with age, was covered in parts with lichen. In some places, the mortar was blackened; in others, it crumbled away from black, yellow and pinky bricks, or red ones roughened from exposure. Halfway down the passage the wall tilted backwards in an arch over a pale blue door, its paint bleached and worn away to pale greyed wood beneath.

Buddleia sprouting out from the wall over their head grew right over the passage, with defiant green leaves beside last summer's crunchy brown dead flowers. Beyond the end of the narrow way through they came upon the river curving up to a large modern bridge.

An old broken lamp-post stood at the edge of the riverside path, which was almost seven feet across, bordered by large slate-coloured bricks, about eighteen inches wide. The wall of Cousin Luke's back garden was over seven feet high, with ugly spikes of glass set into its top.

'Oh, I hate that,' Rachel said at once. 'It's a good thing Matthias is past the climbing age.'

'He certainly means to be private,' her mother replied.

Rachel stepped away on the path to see as much as she could of the house and garden. The darkened red bricks were sombre out of the sun. Summer creepers were now only dry ghostly straws, left hanging on the wall until spring breezes released them or new shoots buried them. Parts of the wall had been strengthened and doubled. They peeped through an old low archway, about five feet high, which had been bricked in, but left some cracks.

The wintry garden was unkempt, forlorn, yet Rachel peering within, exclaimed:

'What a lovely *big* garden! We could grow things there, better than titchy window boxes: All sorts of herbs, if only he'd let us. You'd like fresh mint, chives, parsley, sage and thyme, if he gave me a patch, wouldn't you?'

'Yes, I would. You make me think of Spring,' Mrs David said, sighing to herself without realising it.

Rachel wished that she could cure her mother's sorrow by growing heart's ease, or balm, and giving them to her. She vowed to herself that she would do everything she could with Matthias and Tatiana to make their new home work, if Cousin Luke did make it possible for them to settle in his house. And what wealth it would be to inherit this bare garden, to watch over the transformation of Spring, and encourage the flowering of Summer. For who could foretell what delicate riches might be conjured from this masking soil, if they were given the freedom of his so carefully enclosed patch of land? But all she said to her mother was:

14

'So far, the dock leaves are the greenest thing we've seen. And the river's almost brown.'

The tide was low, and they looked down on to mud and stones, some shingle and old cobbles where once there had been a draw-lock.

'Come on, it's time to meet Cousin Luke, face him in his lair,' Mrs David said, turning abruptly away from the hypnotic flow of the river. 'If we wait any longer, it will make our visit seem even stranger, to me at least. And we mustn't give a bad impression by being late.'

They went back up the passage to the front of the house, and pushed open the tall gate. It swung behind them on a heavy hinge. As it thlonked shut they were cut off from the busy traffic. The noise retreated and they walked slowly up to the looming house, tall above them. The old-fashioned brass bell handle was brilliantly polished, and so was the door knocker.

The door was opened by a small, thin elderly woman. Her iron-grey hair was scraped back into a hard little bun; her skin was yellowy as if she seldom went out of doors. She smoothed down her starched pinafore unnecessarily with little reddened hands, and looked out at them anxiously. Rachel had the feeling that if they spoke too loudly she would jump into the air with fright, then lock and bolt the door in a twinkling. But her mother spoke in her usual pleasant way.

'Good morning. My name is David. I believe that Mr Luke David is expecting me.'

'Yes, madam, he is, madam. If you would like to step in, madam, and you, miss. I will go and see if he is at liberty. Perhaps you would like to take a chair.'

She hurried away, almost at a run, and left them standing in a large entrance hall. There was one small, hard chair beside them on faded carpet, but they stood staring round.

A wide staircase with brown-painted banisters dominated the hall. Rachel nervously counted the nine steps to the curve of the stairs, where a huge black velvet curtain covered the facing wall. It was a gloomy entrance, and she hoped that the upper rooms would be more light and cheerful.

'Would you come this way, please.'

Miss Drube was beckoning to them, and Rachel thought that she had never seen such a white apron, except perhaps in hospital. They followed her into a room, which did not seem to be as big as it was because it was so full of large, heavy furniture, a table with five dining chairs and a carving chair, a roll-top desk, a plum-red chesterfield, small chairs and stands and tables.

At first glance, Rachel thought that the room was empty,

then she saw a thin bony hand appear from behind a high-backed armchair. The long fingers drew together to pick up a large glass marble from a round wooden board, then lift it over another and another. The hand placed a streaked marmalade-yellow marble with a white china one smudged with blue into the curved rim of the board, then retreated.

Miss Drube edged them forward as they hesitated.

'Mr David, sir, your visitors.'

As they came into view Cousin Luke grasped a long chair stick, which was propped against his armchair, ready to stand up, but Mrs David said quickly:

'Please don't get up.'

Cousin Luke inclined his head. He had straight white hair, and looked at them without smiling as he spoke.

'Miss Drube. I shall ring when I need you. Pray sit down. How do you do, Cousin Anna. Good morning, child.'

Rachel thought that Tatiana might have managed a beautiful balletic curtsey, but she merely mumbled: 'Good morning.' She was not sure if she was meant to sit down too, so perched awkwardly on the edge of a small Victorian armchair, holding the end of one of the scrolled wooden arms for support.

Cousin Luke sat bolt upright. As he talked to them he continued to play his marble game, which appeared to work like a sort of draughts, the marbles being lifted away as one jumped over another in his fingers. Rachel was fascinated, watching the glassy and green, shining white, smokey blue, brown balls, as big as the alleys her brother used to collect for the game of marbles. The wooden board was much bigger than a dinner plate, about a foot across.

'Thank you for your letter, Cousin Anna. I shall call you that, and you may call me Cousin Luke. I thought it best that you should see the house for yourself, and judge if what I am prepared to offer would meet your requirements.'

'It's very kind of you,' Mrs David murmured.

Cousin Luke looked up sharply and caught Rachel gazing at the board. 'This is solitaire, child, an old game for a patient brain.'

Rachel said nothing. She wondered if her mother would have a chance to supply her name, but he went on at once:

'Miss Drube claims that she cannot manage the whole house any longer. I fear that if the upper rooms are un-tenanted and neglected the house will suffer. During the war years, I was obliged to let the first and second floors, and they have adequate service rooms, kitchen, bathroom, as you will see. I no longer use them. But I refuse to leave the home of my family, however the surrounding neigh-bourhood is *developed*, *if* such wanton destruction of old properties may be given that name.'

He had raised his voice, and Rachel, startled, looked up at him, then quickly back at her shoes. He spoke as if they had been arguing or ordering him to leave the house.

Mrs David was ill at ease, but cleared her throat and said with brave calm:

'If we accepted your kind offer, we should have to come to some financial arrangement, of course.'

'My solicitor informs me that you have no property of your own?'

'I'm afraid not. You see, we had a London flat supplied by the Company to be convenient for . . .'

'Then you have nowhere to live?' he interrupted.

'Not exactly that. Our present lease is running out, but we could, I expect, find another flat near the children's schools, or else decide to move right away from London,' Mrs David answered proudly.

'This is not London. This is still more of a village, Aynes-combe Green, bounded by the river. I will *not* leave it.' He checked himself, and turned to Mrs David, staring through her rather than at her with cold grey eyes.

'I should not wish to take money from any relation, however distant. You will pay for your own heating, lighting. You will care for the house, as apparently few people are willing to do today, judging from the persons I have

attempted to employ, on Miss Drube's instigation. She will not . . . Miss Drube will show you the back staircase by which the first and second floor may be approached. The back door will be yours alone.'

'But it's too much to take. I mean, we hardly know or knew . . . My husband's father . . .' Mrs David's voice faltered as he coolly began replacing the marbles, each into its little hollow, leaving one empty place in the middle of the thirty-seven. Rachel counted as they went back.

When that was complete, Cousin Luke picked up a small silver bell from the same table, shook it three times, then took hold of his stick. He stood up slowly, and Rachel realised that he was a very tall man, formidably tall standing there, about six feet four, looking down at them, still without smiling. He waited until Miss Drube came, and then said:

'Please show Mrs David upstairs. You may write to me of your decision, Cousin Anna.'

'But I . . .' Mrs David swallowed. 'We do have a piano, and would you call that noise? Or gramophone records?' she added with desperate honesty. 'We are rather keen on music, you see. Wouldn't we disturb you if you've lived here quietly on your own for so long?'

'On my own,' he echoed oddly, and his face twisted a little, though not with the kind of smile Rachel had ever seen before. 'I should not wish you to make *any* noise over this room or the one leading from it, or to use my stairs, but if you used the rooms above these as bedrooms only, I should not be disturbed. If perchance I were, I should of course notify you. Miss Drube will show them to you.'

'But perhaps we should have an agreement, or a trial period, in fairness to both sides,' Mrs David suggested, looking embarrassed.

'Very well. My solicitor will send you an agreement for a trial period of three months, if you decide to accept my proposal. You may write to me. Good morning.'

This, quite clearly, was dismissal. As with some relief she left Cousin Luke, Rachel realised that she had not dared even to mention his garden.

CHAPTER THREE

MISS DRUBE led the way upstairs with little birdy steps.

'What lies behind the big curtain?' Rachel asked, as they reached the curved landing of the staircase they were not to use.

There was no answer, although she knew that she had been heard, for Miss Drube glanced nervously back for an instant. It was an odd reception altogether.

Miss Drube unlocked each door on the first floor, and opened it wide to let Rachel and her mother walk in, standing silently on one side while they looked round. All the rooms were spotlessly clean and shabbily furnished. The narrow kitchen was next door to the bathroom. A large living-room overlooked the back garden and river. Then there were two bedrooms, one large and one small.

The back staircase was fairly narrow and continued to the second floor attic rooms, two small bedrooms, each with an old, hard-looking brass bed, covered, like all the beds, with a thick, white embossed cotton counterpane.

'Acres of room,' Rachel said, peering out of the small windows on to the front of the house. 'These were the maids' bedrooms in the old days, I suppose.'

'They have had two or three living in, and needed it,' Miss Drube commented, leading them across the passage, where a long room stretched right across the back of the house, lit by a high window. Rachel could see out to the river if she stood on tiptoe.

'It all looks beautifully kept,' her mother said warmly. 'What a big house it is for these days.'

'Too big if you ask me. And too much for me at my age. There was a time when I'd have thought nothing of all those stairs, but He . . . still, it's no use complaining. At least it's a home.'

'It could be,' Mrs David said thoughtfully, frowning at the rooms. 'But where is your part, Miss Drube?'

'Down on the ground floor. I've got a pair of rooms to the right of the hall. The kitchen's at the back of the house.'

'Do you look after the garden too?' Rachel asked eagerly.

'No. And he can't get no one to take it on, for love or money.'

'But why? It could be a nice garden. Plenty of people long for a garden, don't they? We have, living in a London flat. We've often wished we could have one, however small.'

'Not this one,' Miss Drube said. 'No one wants to come here. Not with him as he is.' Then she stopped, as if she had accidentally said too much. 'I beg your pardon, ma'am, I'm sure I hope *you'll* be very happy if you do decide to come.'

The emphasis was undoubted, yet they could hardly question her further. Rachel could see that her mother was torn between a desire to know more, and the feeling that she must not encourage Miss Drube to gossip. Cousin Luke had told them so little.

'These rooms have been empty ever since the war then?'

'In a manner of speaking, yes. Mr David did use more rooms at one time, and he inspects the whole house regular, though nowadays he does find it harder to get about, even tap-tapping with that stick of his.'

Rachel thought of him patrolling the empty rooms, check-ing, she supposed, that they were clean, that no one had broken in, then retreating to his own rooms, to quiet, and ticking clocks.

Miss Drube was obviously not willing to leave them alone in the rooms until they were officially tenants, and stood watching them as they walked slowly downstairs again, murmuring to each other.

'Matthias would find the big loft bliss. He could spread all his records and player parts, and have the tape recorder up here too. He could have one of these little bedrooms. Then downstairs, you and Tatiana could share the bigger ones, or else one of you up here and one down.'

'It would be nice to have a bedroom of my own,' Rachel admitted. 'I don't mind one of these attic ones. Then you could have the bigger room. I think you should, anyhow.'

'That's very sweet of you, but, honestly, I shall feel very well off anywhere, if we do take over all this. Tatiana might be happier on the lower floor, as she goes to bed earlier than you. She might feel a bit cut off up there.'

'Whereas we'd like it. And it doesn't disturb *me* if Matthias has a broody mood and plays tapes and electronic bleeps half the night.'

Rachel remembered with a pang how Matthias had played the piano all night after they heard the news of their father's crash. She had got up early, unable to sleep again once the bleak news had come back to her tired mind. Matthias was sitting hunched up at the piano, and all he was able to say was:

'I couldn't go to bed.'

She had brought him coffee and sat with him, saying nothing while he played, repeating time and again one miserable little tune, accompanying it with the harshest discords he could devise. She did not want ever to hear that tune again. Matthias spoke very little about their father. There was little to say. Talking did not always help. He spent more time working at his recordings. There was more time to brood, she knew herself, with the gap left by their father. He no longer breezed in from rehearsals, or ate late suppers, brought them exotic presents from abroad, and free bits and pieces from aeroplanes. Why think of them? She shuddered.

'Don't you think so, Rachel?' her mother was saying, and Rachel returned to Bridge House.

'I'm sorry. I was miles away. What did you say?'

'Just talking to myself really. Working things out,' Mrs David replied, looking briefly at Rachel's white face. She had noticed too how seldom Matthias now was gay. When he wasn't wrapped up in recordings, he only relaxed to tease Tatiana, sometimes mercilessly. It would be wonderful to have a better place to live, an improvement for them all.

'The piano could go in the living-room,' she told Rachel, who blinked hard and with an effort said:

'Yes, of course. That would be fine.'

'We'd have to use the front stairs for that,' Mrs David said, smiling at Miss Drube.

'I suppose he'd let you just the once, if it's one of them big ones,' Miss Drube answered doubtfully, looking slightly alarmed.

'It's a baby grand, and removers couldn't get it up those back stairs, I'm certain. We wouldn't have it over Mr David's room, as you realise.'

'Oh, no,' Miss Drube answered, though she didn't sound convinced. 'He just likes those stairs private. That's his way. I've tried to talk some sense into him scores of times over the years. I've plucked up courage and said what I thought. But all he did was stare through me, and take no notice. He'll never change. I've given up trying. Almost.'

'I quite understand,' Mrs David murmured vaguely, although it was clear to Rachel that she didn't.

They said goodbye to Miss Drube at the back door.

'I hope you will come, madam. It's more than I can stand much longer,' Miss Drube blurted suddenly, then whisked into the house and shut the door.

They walked slowly through the garden and did not speak until they had shut the outer gate.

'Well!' Rachel exclaimed. 'Of all the odd set-ups.' She paused in the street. 'You know what it is about him?'

'What?' Mrs David asked while she tried to banish a suddenly remembered old family nickname, 'Luke the Mule.'

Rachel stood still, stared back at the house, then turned triumphantly to her mother, tossing her smooth brown head of straight hair, so that the black bow shook at the nape of her neck.

'Don't you see. Cousin Luke matches his house!'

'Yes, it is extraordinary,' her mother agreed. 'You can't tell what lies behind those walls and windows.'

'Did you notice she wouldn't tell us what was behind the black curtain?'

'Oh, I don't think she heard you ask. Probably a window, or an old one, bricked in.'

'But they wouldn't tell us lots of things, would they? Didn't you feel that?'

'Yes, I did. He seems to intend to let us live in *his* house, but he isn't exactly welcoming us. He can't be so hard up, or he'd want rent to help in keeping on the place and paying the rates.'

'And he has to pay Miss Drube. And she spoke as if they'd tried to get other people to work there, only nobody would. So he must have been willing to pay them.'

'No, I don't think he's hard pressed,' Mrs David went on. 'I'd always understood from your father that he was quite a wealthy man. There's just something about the house which isn't explained. I don't quite believe that Miss Drube finds it too much, because they're only using the ground floor. It's more than that. *She* seems to want to have us there because she can't stand it any more on her own.'

'She's been there forty years or more, though,' Rachel objected. 'It isn't just her getting older. And it can't be him getting lonely. Because he obviously doesn't want our company. I don't think he likes children. He never *mentioned* the others at all, or even asked my name.'

'I know. But Rachel, however eccentric, it is an offer. And though we're far from beggars, I don't know if we can be choosers, when we want to try and stay near enough your schools, for the next few years if we can, in the most expensive region of England. I must confess too that it would be lovely not to be completely out of touch with the opera and old friends. But that's a luxury.' She hurried on quickly. 'What do you think? I mean if we do get a proper letter from his solicitor offering us the top two floors for three months trial. It does seem we'd be independent.'

'I think we should take it. We needn't see much of him if he's an old misery. We'll be together. That's what we want. Come on, let's find somewhere to have some coffee, because that's what I want!'

'I think we've earned it.'

*   *   *

Matthias and Tatiana were eager to hear news of the visit to Bridge House.

'What's he like?' Tatiana asked.

'Well, it's hard to say after one short meeting,' Mrs David answered diplomatically. 'He seems to be quite clear in his mind about dividing up the house, and giving over the top two floors to us. He didn't seem at all curious about us, as we are about him. Perhaps he's found out all he wants to know from our solicitor and his. He didn't really talk a great deal, did he Rachel?'

'But did you *like* him?' Tatiana insisted.

'And did he like *you*?' Matthias added, with amusement.

'He can't dislike us or he'd hardly be offering us accommodation.'

'What did you think of him, Rachel?'

'He's rather stiff in manner, like his letter,' Rachel said cautiously, trying not to put them off. 'He obviously isn't the kind to gush over you, or anything like that. He looks quite old, perhaps in his seventies, but well preserved, with rather a hard, firm, bony face, a bit like a carving, or sculpture. And he's very tall.'

'Did he show you round, or read out a set of rules for musical tenants?' Matthias asked.

'I don't think he'd thought about music,' said his mother. 'We did mention the piano, and he said it could go over the housekeeper's room, but not his. And she raised no objections, in fact seemed keen for us to come.'

'Very keen,' Rachel put in.

'It was Miss Drube who took us round in fact. Actually, if we accepted it, there'd be heaps of room.'

Mrs David went on to describe the accommodation. As neither of the younger two asked about it, she did not mention their daunting first view of Old Bridge Street and the outside of the house. There would be time for that later. Yet when she had finished, Tatiana seemed to sense that something was being held back.

'I can't really imagine it,' she stated.

'You can usually imagine anything and everything,' Matthias teased her. 'Snakes under the bed and all sorts.'

'No, I don't,' Tatiana denied indignantly. 'That was one dream, once. Why should the housekeeper be more willing than him to have us? It sounds a peculiar household.'

'It may be just his way,' Mrs David replied. 'People do have impulses to help their own family, and he has no closer relations, I believe. Now we've seen it, Rachel and I do think it's worth giving Bridge House a trial, if the solicitor's letter does make a definite offer. But you two can come over with us again this weekend and see for yourselves, before we settle anything.'

'And see him too?'

Mrs David hesitated. 'I think we'd better leave that till later on, Tatiana. It's not fixed up yet.'

'I bet he's an ogre nine feet tall, and you're going to break it to us gently. But we'd still better leave him in his den in peace until we invade *en bloc*. I think from your account, we'd be crazy not to give it a try,' Matthias commented. 'After all, in a year or two, Rachel and I will be earning so much money we'll be able to buy you a house in Park Lane, if you like.'

'No thank you. And I'd rather you took a few more years and trained yourselves properly.'

'Same old story,' Matthias grumbled. 'Wanting us to slave away for more exams as soon as we are shot of schoolwork. An absolute slave driver for a mother, that's what we have. I can see her standing over me threateningly, armed with Cousin Luke's antique pistols, while I fade away out at Aynescombe Green.'

'Hardly, the way you eat. Or the way you've floated through exams so far.'

'So far,' Matthias repeated with mock gloom. 'You'll have to feed me up, that's all. In our new riverside residence!'

Matthias was in favour of Bridge House then, Rachel noted.

'I'll sign on as cook-general indefinitely, if that would help you bear up,' his mother offered.

'Then bring back that cake. I haven't finished eating.'

'Neither have I,' Tatiana said.

Her suspicions about Bridge House seemed to have been completely forgotten. There would be time later to give more details. This, Rachel realised, was the first hurdle passed.

CHAPTER FOUR

A s Cousin Luke had no telephone, Mrs David did as he had asked, and wrote to him. The solicitor's letter presented a very clear agreement for a trial period. All the three children were in favour of the move, and, once they knew they were leaving, the flat seemed unbearably cramped. Tatiana had disliked Old Bridge Street and the gloomy outside of the house in Aynescombe Green, but had been cheered up by promises that she could invite her beloved ballet teacher to visit them as soon as they were settled.

'Miss Julian said she'd heard of Aynescombe Green,' Tatiana told her mother.

'Then it *must* be all right,' Matthias said.

'Of course it will be.' Rachel stepped in hastily.

'Now just be quiet a minute, all of you,' Mrs David said. 'I've written so many letters to Cousin Luke in the last few weeks, I shall soon have permanent writer's cramp. I think I've got everything organised. Gas cooker fixed before one. The things from here in the morning, and the things from storage to arrive this afternoon.'

'What if they bring them here by mistake?' Tatiana asked, spreading golden syrup on toast.

'They won't, cretin,' Matthias said. 'It has all been arranged.'

'You mean you've packed your records and junk.'

'Of course. I wouldn't trust them to anyone else. Particularly a balletic butterfingers not a hundred miles. . . .'

'Finish breakfast,' their mother interrupted. 'It must be washed up and the china put in that last crate by nine o'clock. So eat up without any more arguing, please.'

'As bad as school,' Tatiana muttered.

On the way to Aynescombe Green, Rachel clutched her avocado pear plant, and wondered what sort of reception Cousin Luke would give them. She had not seen him since their first meeting, and her mother had only seen him once more, reporting that he had been as distant and cold as before, merely stating what he expected, and nothing else.

Would he be standing in the hall, keeping a wary eye on his private staircase, or would he retire to his own rooms, away from the possible bustle of the removal men?

In fact, when they reached Bridge House, there was no sign of Cousin Luke. Only Miss Drube appeared when they knocked at the back door.

'It will be all right for the men to use the front stairs for the big pieces?' Mrs David asked. 'Has Mr David said anything about it?'

'Not a word, but that's nothing strange. For him. You'll see for yourselves.'

'What?' Tatiana asked curiously, hearing the end of the conversation and staring first at Miss Drube, then the dim brown hall.

'Nothing to worry about,' Mrs David answered briskly, and quickly introduced Tatiana and Matthias to Miss Drube.

When she met Tatiana, Miss Drube seemed to thaw a little, and offered to help them carry their hand luggage up the back stairs. As they trailed up with the odd treasures not entrusted to the removal van, she noticed Tatiana's best white ballet shoes, sticking out of a shopping basket.

'Going to be a ballyrina, are you?' she asked.

31

'Yes. I am,' Tatiana answered with conviction. 'I wouldn't do anything else.'

'I've seen them on the telly. Very pretty they are too.'

'Then you've got television? Cousin Luke lets you?' Tatiana asked frankly. 'We thought he didn't like it.'

'Nor he doesn't. But I said it was either me going or having the telly, so he gave in, "So long as it does not disturb my studies". I told him I wasn't going to disturb him. And I haven't. But we can't all carry on like him, which is a blessing.'

'How do you mean, carry on?'

'Now stop pestering Miss Drube,' her mother rebuked Tatiana, trying without success to catch her eye, frown and shake her head. Matthias laughed as he dumped a heavy bag down, and Mrs David turned to him with slight exasperation.

'Will you go back downstairs and look out for the van, please? It should be here at any time. They can bring all the crates up our back stairs. Get hold of the big chap before they start, and ask them to be as quiet as they can, will you?'

'Shall I suggest they take off their shoes?' Matthias vanished before she could reply.

'Come on, Tatiana,' Rachel said quickly; 'I'll show you round.'

'I didn't know you had three children, Mrs David. And the little one's going to be a beauty. That blonde hair all done up in a knot. Looks a picture.'

'Yes, she does look after her hair,' Mrs David agreed vaguely. 'Takes hours scragging it up in a chignon neat enough to satisfy her teacher. I think it makes her feel a ballet dancer too, though I admit I like it in plaits best at the moment. She has two lovely thick ones when it's plaited.'

'I braided my hair once.' Mrs Drube hovered in the doorway, obviously not sure whether to go or stay. 'I'll be in the kitchen, Mrs David, if there's anything you need.'

'Thank you. That's very kind of you,' Mrs David replied absently, looking through her handbag for the list she had made in an effort to appear calm, and remember everything in order.

'I hope you'll manage to be happy here, Mrs David. I'm glad you've been able to come. You never know, it might even cheer him up,' Miss Drube added doubtfully. 'Perhaps we'll all be a bit strange when we get to his age.'

'Perhaps we will.' Mrs David was only half listening, as she tried to remember what time the Gas Board had promised to come to connect the cooker.

Miss Drube scuttled off downstairs as Rachel rejoined her mother.

'Tatiana's not sure if she wouldn't like Matthias' room as a studio. She says she could put up a *barre* and do exercises. There'd be room to leap about and so on.'

'No! That room's for Matthias. He'll need the space for his equipment, and a retreat from a household of women!'

'There's Cousin Luke, don't forget.'

'I don't know how we'll count him. We'll have to see. Look out of the window. Any sign of the men?'

'Yes. Matthias is showing them the way to the back door.'

'Oh good. Now all the crates and boxes are labelled, so it should be straightforward.'

'Of course it will be. You've got everything organised beautifully,' Rachel assured her. 'We'll be straight in no time.'

The men were friendly and cheerful, even when they realised that the whole load had to be carried to the first and second floors. Rachel and her mother charmed them, guided them and thanked them. Matthias helped the two men with awkward pieces, scowling over the heavy weights,

33

his straight black hair flapping into his eyes as he heaved and lifted. Tatiana had changed into flat ballet shoes, and pranced around, looking into corners and swinging round at the top of the stairs, arching her leg, extending her foot, while balancing with her hand on the banister, humming with tremulous excitement.

Rachel could not feel excited. She felt it was a grey and mercifully busy day. When she was a little girl, things had been so much less complicated: black when her father was away, shining white on his returns, when they cajoled late bedtimes and he talked for what seemed hours. He had talked on till the children were willing to fall into bed, and hear his rich voice rising and falling, his singing laugh echoing through the flat. Her mother used to glow as she listened to him. Rachel glanced at her, busy unwrapping china from its newspaper cocoons.

'There isn't much more, is there?' Mrs David asked.

Tatiana darted into the kitchen, then out on to the main landing, looking down into the big hall.

'Only a few pictures, I think.'

'Funny that Cousin Luke didn't come and watch them bring the piano up *his* stairs,' Tatiana said. 'I loved the way they unscrewed the legs.'

'I expect he was glowering at them through his keyhole,' Matthias said, coming into the kitchen. 'What on earth's that?'

He rushed to the back stairs and Tatiana to the landing, as an enormous crash echoed through the house. It seemed to go on for a long time, as if a load of china had tumbled in slow motion down hard, wooden stairs. Mrs David, appalled, followed Matthias, but Rachel went out on to the landing.

She saw that Tatiana was standing at the top of the main staircase in a strangely mesmerised attitude, as if caught in

34

a pose she could not change, leaning round the banister to gaze downwards, one foot curving over the first step.

Cousin Luke was tapping his way across the hall, and came to stand at the foot of the stairs.

'What was broken? And what is the meaning of this hideous noise? What are you doing there, child? How dare you crash about on that staircase. I made it perfectly clear that I will *not* have children rampaging over the whole house.'

'I wasn't doing anything. I just . . .'

Rachel joined her sister, who was trembling with fright as the old man glared up at her. Although they were above him, somehow his height looked threatening.

'I'm sorry, Cousin Luke. There was an accident. Something was dropped on the *back* stairs. Not here at all. But we've nearly finished. And we won't be disturbing you again.'

'I sincerely trust that you will not. And I do *not* wish you to use these stairs in the future. You understand too, child?'

He raised his stick to point it at the petrified Tatiana, who just nodded, and watched dumbly as he walked back across the hall into his room.

Only when the door was shut did she relax and look at Rachel with widened eyes.

'But he's *horrible*. You didn't tell me that. I hate him.'

'No you don't,' Rachel said soothingly. 'He was just a bit cross, that's all.'

'He wasn't. He was angry, not even hot angry — cold and horrible. And frightening.'

'Now then, don't exaggerate. He's just funny about his old stairs in *his* house. Come on, let's see what they've managed to drop down *ours*!'

She hustled Tatiana back into the kitchen, where Matthias was carefully picking up fragments of glass which had fallen between the frames and the pictures, then adding them to a mass of shattered glass collected in a dust pan.

'Watch your fingers for splinters,' Mrs David warned him. 'It's fantastic how much glass comes from one picture.'

'This was two,' one of the men said. 'I am that sorry, ma'am. It was my fault entirely, trying to take the two together, with them being different sizes and all. Just slipped through my fingers.'

'Never mind; we're insured. And it might have been much worse.'

'It sounded like a crate of glasses at least!' Matthias said. 'Marvellous sound effects.'

'You see, I caught the one frame at the top of the stairs. I don't know what I was up to. Not like me at all. Must be losing my grip.'

'No, you're just tired,' Mrs David told the crestfallen removal man. 'We'll all have a cup of tea straightaway, as Miss Drube's very kindly lent me an electric kettle.'

They sat round the table and drank tea. Mrs David dug out a box of biscuits, and it felt quite festive until Rachel looked across at Tatiana, staring into space with tear-bright eyes, her hands clasped round her hot mug, as if to gain reassurance from its warmth.

CHAPTER FIVE

THEY all worked hard to settle into their new home, although Mrs David did most of the work as it was still term time for their first days at Aynescombe Green.

On the last day of her term, Rachel broke up at twelve o'clock. As usual, she went with a group of girl friends to a nearby coffee bar to celebrate the beginning of the holidays, but somehow, this time, for her the party fell flat. The other girls were planning meetings and outings, tennis and swimming, window-shopping. They all lived near to each other, could cycle or walk, take a short bus ride. She so missed gossiping on the phone, endless discussions of new clothes. She now lived a tube and a train journey away from them all, more than an hour's journey, whose fare she could not afford, once her school pass ended. It had proved a long and tiring day to travel to school from Aynescombe Green, and, though she knew she would get used to it, as thousands of commuters did, it now seemed wearisome.

She looked at the bright coffee bar, with its gaudy lights, and suddenly longed quite hopelessly for the past. In other holidays, she and her friends had met most days. They had been to rehearsals at the opera, out to lunch with her father, but it was no use thinking of that. In this holiday, she had a depressing feeling that she would be almost imprisoned with Matthias and Tatiana, the unwilling buffer between the worst of their quarrels, when ballet and music exploded within Bridge House. Their father had managed to send them packing with great aplomb, shouted them down, quite literally. And she missed that too.

Rachel stood up to shake away the spate of memories, quickly made an excuse and said goodbye. The only way to tackle the new house was to make it work for them as a family. Then they could welcome friends for visits. Her mother was right. She forced her mind into positive plans all the way back, and was not even dismayed when she reached Bridge House and found her mother out, presumably shopping. Rachel decided to go out into the garden and prepare a bed for herbs. The afternoon was fine, and it was a good excuse to be out of doors. She left by the back door with a small trowel and wandered round the garden. It was forlornly neglected, and she imagined that Cousin Luke would have no objection to a little cultivation there. She was not sure where to start, and returned to an old flower bed back at the side of the house. It would be sheltered here, and quite sunny, and near the back door for her mother to use, if the herbs really thrived. In its heyday, the garden would have been tended by a proper gardener, nurtured with care from season to season. The bed was tangled with weeds so she knelt down and set to work.

Nearby, at the back corner of the house there was a small shuttered window, which they had never seen open. It intrigued them all. Matthias had invented some splendid interiors to tease Tatiana, or make his mother laugh. Now, as she worked, Rachel was surprised to hear the clank of a metal bar, and clonking of wood as the shutters were, she supposed, folded back. The sound of a window bar being notched came next, she decided, and she sat back on her heels, intensely curious, though not daring to look round the corner to see into the shuttered room.

The next moment, she was glad that she had not moved,

because Cousin Luke's voice came clearly out to the quiet garden.

'This is quite unnecessary, Miss Drube.'

'The room needs an airing, Mr David, sir. I doubt that you could tell me when you last had this window open. The fresh air won't hurt it. It couldn't do no harm, now could it, a lovely day like this?'

'Miss Drube. I am not prepared to discuss the matter. Kindly do what cleaning is needful, and give your attention to keeping everything in its proper place. I do not wish there to be any change. And I wish you to have completed this work as soon as possible, so that I may continue my work without interruption.'

Miss Drube was obviously not going to be silenced. Perhaps she was affected by Spring, Rachel thought, and had a wild vision of Miss Drube's neat grey head crowned with a ridiculous hat of feathers and imitation Easter eggs.

'The family upstairs must think it a bit queer, keeping these shutters drawn all the time.'

'Miss Drube, the conduct of my affairs is no concern of theirs, or of yours.'

'Of course not, sir,' Miss Drube answered nervously, 'I only meant that naturally, they might wonder. The little girl is a friendly little mite and was just asking. . . .'

'I forbid you to discuss my apartments with that child or anyone else. I have made it abundantly clear that I will not tolerate intrusion. Mrs David's family have been given accommodation as a matter of duty, and only on the condition that I am not disturbed; and I include the prying of an inquisitive child. Nothing is to be altered downstairs. Nothing.'

'Well, sir,' Miss Drube replied with a spirit Rachel couldn't help admiring, as she herself was wilting on the path at the icy tone he used; 'Things are altered upstairs,

I must say. And much for the better. It's alive up there, and I, for one, am glad of it.'

'Miss Drube, you forget yourself and your position. I shall come back to lock this room in half an hour, and shall be obliged if you would complete your work in that time.'

His stick tapped. A door was shut and Rachel breathed out hard.

'What an extraordinary old man he is! He seems almost frightened of associating with us. I must tell Matthias about this.'

*   *   *

She did not find an opportunity until late that evening, when she went into Matthias' big attic room opposite hers. He heard the story through without comment, as he sat at a table working to re-connect their father's tape recorder.

'He's a funny old devil. But I think Miss Drube's taken on a new lease of life since we've come here, even if he hasn't.'

'That's Tatiana. Miss Drube dotes on her. She goes into her kitchen and cadges a view of any ballet on television.'

Matthias grinned. 'She hasn't asked *me* to visit her in her parlour. She seems scared of me. Perhaps the old man's put her off males. What do you think of him? Do you dislike him, Rachel?'

'It's hard to say. I feel I don't know him properly. So does Mummy. But he doesn't seem to intend that we should get to know him. Tatiana's frankly scared of him since that outburst on the day we moved.'

'Oh, she's just a silly kid,' Matthias replied unsympathetically, 'though he is a dislikeable old misery. He can still get about, but does he ever go out anywhere?'

'Yes, he goes to some Library or something, every Monday, Tuesday and Friday. Miss Drube told Tatiana; she talks a lot to her. She doesn't gossip to Mummy much, just is friendly in a guarded sort of way when we three are out, as if she's relieved to have someone else in the house.'

'Half scared of what the old man'll say. You didn't see into the shuttered room at all?' asked Matthias, intent on his intricate leads.

'No thank you. I kept well out of sight.'

'I wonder what it is? A hoard of treasure? Stolen property from international museums he sits and gloats over? A body in an old oak chest?'

'I'm not Tatiana. You can't scare me. But don't overdo it with her, will you, Matthias? She's already got some idea that there is something strange about Cousin Luke, and it really frightens her. We don't want her put off the house when we're trying to settle here.'

'But there *is* something odd, isn't there? He *is* hiding something.'

'Yes, it's puzzling. I don't dislike him exactly. I feel sorry for him in a way. He's sort of cut off, and I'd like to reach him.'

'I thought you were going to be a nurse, not a psychologist,' Matthias said, laughing at her.

'Well, did I tell you what they said to me in the newsagent's when I went to order papers?'

'No. What?'

'The woman said: "The old gentleman's gone then?" So I said: "Oh no, we're in the top flat. He's still downstairs", and she said: "I beg your pardon. I thought he must have passed away since someone else was living there. I own I am surprised. He's a funny one. Never taken a paper or a weekly since we had this business. And that house has quite a name in this neighbourhood. It's never been a happy house. But if there's the three of you with your mum, maybe you young ones will make all the difference." '

'Cheery,' Matthias commented. 'She must be the village gossip. All information to be taken with a large pinch of salt. Anyhow, one thing we have got here is space. I've never been able to get my stuff arranged like this before.'

'What are you doing?' Rachel looked at the array of tapes and the tape recorder with its knobs and black finger switches, marked Start, Fast, Wind, Stop, Pause. They were all mysteriously complicated to her, however patiently Matthias tried to explain them.

'It's something I'm trying out. What intrigues me is *how* the sound is produced, then reproduced. And how you can alter it, and mix it, in different ways.'

He became absorbed in showing her how the playback worked, how you measured the speed of the tape's movement in inches per second.

Rachel watched and nodded and listened, taking in all she could. It was a relief to concentrate on listening: it was a respite from thinking about their precarious situation in the house of Cousin Luke.

*   *   *

The following day, Rachel and her mother went to visit Cousin Luke's solicitor. He was a small, elderly man, with a stiffened white wing collar and pince-nez. He spoke in a soft Scottish voice, with the greatest politeness.

'It is most kind of you, Mrs David, to come to call on me at my office, and I hope that you have not found the journey fatiguing.'

'Not at all, thank you. It was perfectly straightforward. My daughter's an expert commuter already.'

'You are all finding yourselves comfortable, I trust?'

43

'Yes, thank you. Mr Murdoch.' Mrs David hesitated. 'I may speak in confidence?'

'Mrs David, you can rely absolutely on my discretion.'

'Then can you tell us any more about Cousin Luke, without, of course, invading professional privacy? You see we are all rather bewildered. He is letting us live in his house, rent free, yet it seems he can hardly bear the sight of us.'

'Oh, I'm sure that is not the case. Mr Luke David has, I consider, a strong sense of duty. He has given you this help because you are part of his family.'

'A rather remote part.'

'And he doesn't seem interested in *us* at all,' Rachel added. 'We haven't rushed at him or anything, but he's positively scared my young sister by his prickliness.'

'I am sorry to hear that, because I do feel that it is better that Mr David should not continue to live in such complete solitude. I have thought so for some years. In fact, I think I can reveal to you that Miss Drube came to me in great distress on more than one occasion, because she found the work so lonely, but did not wish to desert him.'

'But he could have afforded other help presumably,' Mrs David said, 'although I know it's not easy to find nowadays.'

Mr Murdoch paused, as if to choose his words with care.

'I cannot tell you why other people have refused to stay at the house. Mr David is a complex person, and, as you will know, he endeavours to cut himself off from modern life, the wireless, the television, the telephone. But there is some other barrier there, which perhaps, and this I sincerely hope, a young family may break through, with perseverance.'

'If he wants it,' Mrs David said doubtfully. 'You see, it's so strange. I feel grateful, and it is a tremendous help, but approaching him is like walking into a stone wall.'

44

'With spiky glass on top,' Rachel put in, wincing. 'Did you know Mrs David?' she asked on impulse. Her mother shook her head and began to speak, but Mr Murdoch answered with deliberation.

'I did meet Mrs David, although she was not directly my client.'

'And what was she like?'

'Mrs David was one of the most beautiful young women I have ever seen. Perhaps because I was young myself then, and more susceptible—' he twitched at his pince-nez with amusement at his own little witticism. 'But she was fair, very fair and young, and quite lovely. The natural English rose. It was a very sad circumstance.'

'That she ran away?' Rachel prompted, deliberately not catching her mother's eye, knowing that she was being frowned at for asking so many questions.

'Yes, it was, I understand, a trivial quarrel. I never knew the cause. But she ran away and he refused to ask her to return, refused to trace her in any way.'

'And that was all? He just let her go?'

'As I understand it. But solicitors are not always given all the facts, Miss David.'

'And neither are inquisitive girls,' Mrs David added. 'The truth is, Mr Murdoch, that we are grateful for this accommodation, and wonder if you had asked us here to suggest some form of payment?'

'By no means. I merely asked you to call for my own reassurance and satisfaction, being well aware that the situation is an unusual one. Mr David is also greatly attached to the house itself in a manner which is perhaps somewhat unusual.'

'Oh, we don't think it's haunted or anything,' Rachel told him frankly. 'It may not have been a happy house. We've had gloomy hints from local people. But we're not going to

45

be superstitious. I don't think you should be in these days, do you?'

'I do not imagine that lawyers have ever been so, to any large degree,' he answered dryly. 'But it is my sincere hope that you and your family will bring something of the twentieth century into that home, Miss David.'

'We will. You should hear some of my brother's recordings. They sound like the twenty-first century at least. Still, Cousin Luke hasn't complained yet, if he can hear them down there.'

'I must confess that I seldom venture beyond the nineteenth century for my musical relaxation,' Mr Murdoch admitted, 'but perhaps I am too old to change.'

'I think Cousin Luke may be,' Mrs David said quietly. 'But he has been kind to us in his way, and, if ever he gives *you* the chance, would you please tell him that we appreciate it.'

CHAPTER SIX

RACHEL was in the garden again. It was bright and fresh, and she had decided to cut off the last year's dead flowers, which still straggled in parts of the garden, ugly amongst so much sprouting green. Tatiana came out and stood watching her.

'Do you like it here, Rachel?'

'Better than squashed in that flat. Mummy hasn't missed her kitchen scissors yet, has she?'

'I don't know. Rachel, you're not listening.' Tatiana flung her single heavy plait angrily over her shoulder. 'Can't you stop snipping at those hideous brown things for one minute?'

'Why?' Rachel asked calmly. 'I can hear just as well while I do this. What's the matter? Have you been rowing with Matthias, lost the battle and come to take it out on me? I'm not fighting, just enjoying the sun while it's here.'

'Don't be mean. I haven't *seen* Matthias this morning. He's in his room. I wanted to talk to you about the house.'

'Talk on then.' Rachel knew that she was maddening Tatiana, who was turning on one leg, whipping the other in irritable *fouettés*. But she had been so content to be out of doors and on her own, thinking of an old remedy she had read of, for a bad cough in March, that if you were to spit on a frog's head it would carry your cough away. She glanced up at Tatiana, but saw she was not going to be amused by that, or anything else, until smoothed out.

47

'All right, what is the trouble?' she asked, as so often before.

'Rachel, *do* you like this house? Really?'

'How do you mean, like? I think we're lucky to be here. We can all be together and at our schools and classes. . . .'

'I know all that. You and Mummy have said it *dozens* of times, but I'm scared of it, and of *him*. I'll *never* be happy here.'

'Of course you will. It's just strange to you, that's all.'

'No, it's not that. There's something wrong with the house. Miss Drube thinks so too.'

'Now look here, Tatiana. You mustn't believe everything everyone tells you. Superstitions flourish when people are old and odd, as Cousin Luke is, I admit. And, when he was young, this was more of a village, and gossip thrives in a village. This is an old house, left rather isolated when so much has been pulled down. You've probably heard old tales altered by scores of tellings, elaborated during the years. Miss Drube has been here for about forty years, hasn't she and . . .'

'This is fact,' Tatiana stated defiantly, standing with her feet flattened on the path. 'You know the walled passage at the side of the house?'

'Of course.'

'Well, it used to be a notiorous, I mean notorious, runway for smugglers and river thieves.'

'That's not surprising, but it doesn't affect us today, except it's interesting to know.'

'But even then this house was unlucky.' Tatiana paused dramatically, then went on when Rachel did not react. 'It's always been unlucky, since stolen things were hidden here. And it's always been the women of the family who have been the unlucky ones.'

'You've been making things up, just to scare yourself,' Rachel told her.

'No, I haven't. And I won't tell you what Miss Drube said about Cousin Luke's wife now, if you don't believe me.'

'I don't believe in "luck", good or bad, and I think people often frighten themselves into feebleness by saying something is "unlucky". It harms them, because they give in to what was bad in the past, and don't give the present a fair chance. It's not a healthy way to think.'

'I don't know what you mean.' Tatiana was piqued by Rachel's lack of curiosity. 'I thought you wanted to know about his wife.'

'I do, *if* you know anything.'

'Miss Drube said their quarrel was about something unlucky in the house. I haven't found out exactly what it was, but Mrs David — she was called Amelia — wanted to get rid of it. And he wouldn't. So she ran away. That's all I've wheedled out of Miss Drube *so far*. But the house is *still* unlucky.'

'Rubbish!' Rachel said energetically. 'That sounds a real old wives' tale, old spinster's tale, to be accurate. You've been on at her so much, she's made it up to please you. She'll be providing you with a ghost next, if you're not careful! Miss Drube is rather a nervous person, you know, and she's been lonely all these years, looking after an almost empty house.'

'Well, why does he keep us from seeing his part of the house? He *is* hiding something.'

'Not necessarily. I think he's just hugging his privacy. After all, he's been on his own for all these years. It's a habit. Honestly, Tatiana, I think you ought to be more reasonable. He may have given us accommodation out of a sense of duty, but he may not want us over-running the whole place. If we can gradually get him to accept us as people, so much the better.'

'He hates me,' Tatiana declared. 'The way he looks at me. His eyes are like a snake's.'

'You do exaggerate.'

'I'll find out more when he's out and then perhaps you'll believe me. I'll prove it to you.'

'I shouldn't nose round. It's not fair,' Rachel answered seriously. 'And you mustn't worry Mummy with all this either. You can tell me,' she added more gently, 'but I'm sure there's nothing to be frightened about.'

'But Rachel, there may not be a ghost, but there are sounds in the night. I've heard them.'

'What sounds?'

'Music, in the distance.'

'That would be Matthias, you ninny. He's only one floor over your bedroom.'

'No, it's not his records, or the piano, I'm positive. It's sort of high, a tinkling tune, a long way away. I don't know what, but it woke me up, and it was the middle of the night. It stopped before I could place the tune.'

'I'm sure it would be Matthias. He's always recording bits and pieces on tape, and he does often stay up much later than you. Or it could have been Miss Drube's television.'

'I don't think so.' Tatiana was unconvinced.

Rachel realised that she was genuinely distressed. 'Then you can wake me up if you hear it again. You may have dreamt it — the dance of the Sugar Plum Fairy! Don't get upset now about Bridge House. After all, it's given you your chance to stay on with Miss Julian. I think we would definitely have had to leave London otherwise; we couldn't have afforded a decent place. Is she having holiday classes this Easter, by the way?'

'Yes. Mummy says I can go up twice a week. I'd like to. I don't want to get stiff. And we're going to have some of the American Company who are doing a London season. They may come to our classes then I'll actually see them.' Tatiana's face had changed completely, no longer pinched, but alive with enthusiasm.

'That'd be marvellous. It's always rather odd to me to think that the famous ballerinas sweat away for hours at the *barre* every day doing exercises just like you.'

'Not quite. They do them a bit better!' Tatiana smiled for the first time, and perked up like a bird about to fly into the blue. 'But I'm working like mad so that she will let me go forward for the finals of a scholarship to Ballet School this year. If I got there, I'd be so happy I'd live in a hovel!'

She danced off up the path, her fears and gloom

apparently forgotten as she curved towards her shadow, then twirled round so that her plait swirled out from her head before she vanished indoors.

Rachel returned to her snipping, smelling the fresh earth and glad to watch the new life burgeoning even in this neglected garden. A single shining yellow crocus caught her eye, opening wide to the sun, proudly showing its golden stamens inside. It was lovely to have a garden.

Her peace was shortlived. She heard a tapping behind her and turned to see Cousin Luke coming down the path. She scrambled to her feet, startled and apprehensive, in spite of herself and her good common sense when talking to Tatiana.

'What are you doing?'

'I was just tidying up. I mean, just cutting off a few dead flowers. It seemed a pity and I like gardens and — I hope you don't mind. . . .' Rachel gabbled stupidly, and stopped in confusion. He really did fix his eye upon you, and he never seemed to change expression. It was a good thing Tatiana had gone, though that didn't help her situation, standing clutching kitchen scissors.

'It was once a beautiful garden,' Cousin Luke remarked. 'My mother tended it herself when she and the house were alive.'

'You wouldn't mind then,' Rachel dared to ask after this odd remark, 'if I planted a few herbs, and cleared out the dead wood and so on? It'd give the new shoots a chance.'

'You can't get rid of past years as easily as that. You may tidy if you wish, but I do not want the house or garden changed in my lifetime. I shall make my record of it all. It has been a beautiful house and that will be the end of it, for me and my family.'

'But gardens don't end,' Rachel protested. 'That's one of the reasons I like them. They keep on growing and renewing themselves. Every year. You must have seen after the war how the deserted bomb sites became wild gardens. The weeds grew green over the scars and healed them, covered over the rubble with grass and dandelions and bright pink Rose Bay Willow Herb. My mother told me about it, and how people called it London Pride. I loved that. We even found an old bomb site, a little one, only the other day, but the bull-dozers were going to break through to start a new building.'

'They may do that here when I am gone,' Cousin Luke said. 'This age is full of destruction. But for my lifetime it will stay the same. Once there was genuine London Pride here, but I expect it was smothered by weeds years ago.'

'I'll look out for it and rescue it if I find it,' Rachel promised.

'I did not think that young people today interested themselves in gardening,' Cousin Luke said, leaning on his stick, and looking at Rachel. 'Only in noise and public disturbance, dressed in extraordinary clothes.'

'Perhaps you don't know enough young people,' Rachel suggested boldly, encouraged by their first real conversation, and hoping that he was not referring to her rather tight old jeans, in which Matthias claimed she bulged.

Cousin Luke did not choose to answer, and looked through her reflectively before he turned and walked slowly back towards the house. Yet Rachel felt that she had made a start. She turned back to the garden, and, after a short search, found a carpet of sprigs almost hidden away in a corner. The little clusters of leaves with rounded scallops were like open, bright green roses. A few leaves were dark red, and she knew that she had tracked down the London Pride. So she cleared the weeds from that patch and freed the shoots to grow without hindrance. If they were still living there in the summer, she would pick some of the

53

delicate pink flowers and take them in to Cousin Luke.

She loved soft pink, and sat back on the path, dreaming of frothy pink ball dresses, dancing with medical students, transformed from her starchy nurse's uniform, and dull everyday appearance. That was if she managed to pass her exams. Rachel wished that she could flash through them with ease, as Matthias seemed to do. Still, it was some help not to change schools just when work was going to be so important.

'If only Cousin Luke stands the trial period. And our dancing Tatiana too!'

CHAPTER SEVEN

DURING the next few days of the holidays, the Davids established what Matthias called a piano-forte way of life. Everyone was quiet and careful, *pianissimo* on the first-floor landing, when they knew that Cousin Luke was at home. During his absences, they relaxed, called through the house to each other, played the wireless, the piano and the record player as they wished. And it was possible to gauge exactly what was permissible, for Cousin Luke kept to a strict routine. On Monday, Tuesday and Friday, he left the house at nine thirty and returned at two o'clock.

'You could set your watch by him,' Miss Drube told the three of them. 'Been doing it for years.'

'Where does he go?' In spite of her dislike, Tatiana was fascinated by the old man. The whole family was, in some measure. For even when he was away, they were conscious that he would be coming back, that their exuberant noise would have to be subdued and curtailed.

'He goes to some Library in the town. In London. It's a tidy way, up in Kensington, I think. All to do with his writing. And I don't know what that is. History or something, but I suppose it keeps him happy.'

'Happy!' Tatiana's voice ascended to a peak of scorn. 'He doesn't know the meaning of the word. Matthias calls him a miserable old devil and I think he's right.' She avoided her brother's glare while Rachel added quickly:

'That was not intended for repetition, Tatiana. I'm sorry,

Miss Drube. It's just that we always used to live rather a busy life, and, as my father was a singer, he often practised at home. We're used to a lot of music, almost non-stop all day. And sometimes it's an effort to be as quiet as my mother thinks we should be, to fit in with him. It seems negative, just *not* making a noise. But we don't want to be rude about Cousin Luke in front of you. Tatiana, you might say you're sorry.'

'I'm not, though. Only sorry we have to live with him. And he *is* an old misery. Glum! When did you ever see him smile?'

'Perhaps he doesn't like the way you hold your nose?' Matthias suggested; 'Or the way you point your toes.'

'Oh stop it!' Tatiana rushed out of the room almost in tears, and Rachel sighed. The holidays were less easy than term time in some ways. She herself felt walled in at times, particularly on wet days like today, when she dreaded Cousin Luke's oppressive invisible presence below them, imposing his wishes, with which they were bound to comply, as tenants on charity. She had come to the conclusion reluctantly that he was tolerating them entirely out of a sense of duty. Perhaps they would remain like this, sharing his house but in no way entering his life.

Obviously, they couldn't force their way in. He was merely a distant relation: they had no claim on him, his house or his time. But her whole feeling was that there should be a means of meeting him, some common ground, some way of healing the breach. If she were honest with herself, she hated living in the same house on such poor terms with Cousin Luke. And she suspected that her mother felt equally depressed and helpless at times. He so clearly did not wish to communicate more than necessary. Already Mrs David was talking of hopes for a move elsewhere when she and Matthias had left school.

56

But that left acres of time at Bridge House. Rachel turned her hypnotised eyes from the grey rain.

'I'm sorry, Miss Drube,' she repeated with an effort. 'Tatiana does get worked up. She doesn't mean all she says.'

'Don't worry. I was young myself once. A long time ago.'

Rachel blinked at the unexpected small joke. Miss Drube, at least, had thawed out, and that was largely due to Tatiana's bursts of love and hate. They all knew that, and Rachel was not surprised when Miss Drube asked:

'I was wondering, Rachel, if your mother would let me take Tatiana out for a treat. Just the two of us. She's set her heart on the London Museum, and I've never been there. It would be an outing for us both, and I couldn't tell you when I last took the day off. I did just mention it to Mr David,' she finished in a nervous little rush.

'And did the old man say: "No, a thousand times no, I'd far rather die than say yes"?' Matthias asked.

'He just said: "If you so wish, Miss Drube, I have no objection."'

Her quaint imitation of Cousin Luke's precise manner made them both laugh, and they felt that Miss Drube in her way was on their side. Rachel was slightly cheered, and decided that it might even stop raining before the holidays ended. And it was Monday, so Cousin Luke would be going out later on.

'Good morning, Miss Drube. I suppose the gardens need all this, but I must admit I'd prefer it not to come down in buckets.'

'Good morning, Mrs David. I was wondering . . .' Miss Drube stopped shyly, and smoothed her white apron.

'Mummy. Miss Drube would like to take Tatiana to the London Museum for a holiday treat. She's got the day off, if you agree.'

'That's very kind of you, Miss Drube. I'm sure Tatiana would be delighted. She wants to see the model theatres there, I know, and we've never got round to it. When do you suggest?'

Miss Drube looked baffled. 'Well, today, if it's convenient? Because he might change his mind by tomorrow. You never know.'

'That would be lovely. I know there's no class today. She hasn't anything else on, has she, Rachel?'

'Just a temperament,' Matthias muttered.

'She threw a bit of a scene, that's all, but I'll go and find her,' Rachel said. 'I think she'd like an outing.'

'Say she's got to wear wellingtons though,' Mrs David called after Rachel. 'We can lend you a big umbrella, if you like, Miss Drube, then you won't get drowned on your way to the station. Where is it, Matthias?'

'In my room,' Matthias answered stiffly. His teasing gaiety had gone, and he looked sullen and miserable: he did not want to lend his father's huge black umbrella, under which they had walked to and from the theatre, talking about music and singing and sound and noise.

'Perhaps it will ease up,' Mrs David said, after a quick glance at him. 'What time would you like Tatiana to be ready?'

'Any time now. Then you see we could have some dinner out, and come back before the rush hour. Would that be all right?' Miss Drube asked anxiously. 'I'd take great care of her, Mrs David.'

'Of course you will. She's a lucky girl to be given a treat on a day like this.'

Miss Drube went back downstairs, and Mrs David handed a letter to Matthias.

'One for you and one for me. Isn't that Viv's handwriting?'

58

'Looks like it,' Matthias answered shortly, and slit open the letter with a small screwdriver he kept in his jacket pocket.

'Nice to have letters,' Mrs David went on: 'But if we do settle here with Cousin Luke — I mean if he puts up with us — I'll persuade him to let me apply for a 'phone. Letters aren't the same. I think we all feel a bit cut off from our friends at times. We're just ruined these days. Letters seem slow in comparison.'

'They certainly do,' Matthias replied, smiling a little to himself and at last looking up from his own letter. He had only half listened to what his mother said.

'You look pleased. Was it Viv? What did he say?'

'I'm intrigued. And I can't tell you for the moment. I haven't taken it all in myself yet.'

'All right.' Mrs David was glancing through her own letter and exclaimed:

'How lovely. Do you think I could?'

'Could what?'

'Go up to the Opera House today.'

'Why not?'

'Well, there's lunch to think of and . . .'

'Don't be such a mother hen. Tatiana's going out and Rachel and I'll be fine. I'm going to test something while the old man's out. I've borrowed a squeaker from a boy at school. Who's asked you anyhow?'

'Tim. He's giving a small lunch party for some visitors from Italy, and he was going to 'phone me, then realised that we weren't on the 'phone. So he sent this scrawl yesterday.'

'You go.'

'Go where?' Rachel had come back.

'Out to lunch with Tim. It'd do her good to get a break from looking after Cousin Luke's precious house, wouldn't it? You haven't been to London since we came here, have you?'

'No. Well, I've been busy and . . .'

'You thought *you* should settle down too,' Rachel added. 'So you deserve a break. And it'll be a super lunch too. Daddy always said that Tim was such a successful manager because he lured the singers out to large lunches, then persuaded them to do just what he wanted when he'd got them into a good temper.'

'All right then, I'll go,' Mrs David said. 'I really don't need much persuading!'

'Dress up too,' Rachel told her. 'Wear your black and white dress.'

'I'll see.'

Mrs David hovered, looking through the letter again until Rachel said:

'We'll wash up breakfast. You go and get glammed up. I'm going to garden, if it stops raining, and Matthias is going to blast off the attic roof while Cousin Luke is out. So we'll be quite happy. You have a holiday.'

As soon as Mrs David was out of earshot, Matthias said:

'You won't be gardening this morning. We've something to do. Look at this.'

He handed her his letter, closely typewritten in blue.

Dear Matthias,

I hope you all four are well. We must arrange a meeting during the Easter, so-called holidays, but life has been unusually chaotic and busy even for us, ever since we got back last week from South Africa. Jane and I did a joint examination tour, so we were able to cut the time down to three months, but it was hard going. We had a great welcome home from Alistair and Sarah.

I know that the duty of a godfather is to cough up

good presents for his godson's birthday, but will you, for this once, help me to get a special one to your mother? Quite by chance, (in our usual way) we came across a pair of street pianos, languishing irresistibly in an old circus owner's stables. I admit we have kept the better of the two. (Sarah insisted is my excuse.) But even we have to admit that we can't house two. So we'd like to give it to your mother for her birthday, and you to get it into the flat and hidden beforehand, if possible. I know it may be a bit of a squash till you do find a larger place, but we couldn't resist sending it now. It may need some small adjustment. See for yourself. I'm sending a copy of a talk on mechanical instruments to guide you, but I'm confident you can cope if you can manage all those tapes you delight in.

I'm sure your mother will like it. Ours has an incredible tone, juicy in the extreme. You'll have to send her out while you try it! Tried to 'phone you but no answer, so I'm sending this letter to give you warning that the street piano will be delivered to you between twelve and one next Monday. Do try and keep it hidden, if you can!

Will be in touch. Love from us all to you all.

As ever,

Viv.

P.S. If you have any trouble with this bolt from the blue, think of us. Our two have become fascinated by an absurd invention, patented in 1854 by Daniel Hewitt, of a piano without a frame, whose strings were merely attached to the wall of the house. I'm only surprised we didn't come home to find one 'up'. And, before you think of parading your present, and it's really for you all, be warned by Professor Babbage, who invented the Calculating Machine. In the first six months of 1861, he was so maddened by his work being interrupted by six brass bands and ninety-six street pianos and organs in only ninety days that he spent over a hundred pounds on prosecuting the musicians. Alistair dug that up for me, so be careful you're not pursued by the irate scholars of north London. V.B.

Rachel handed back the letter.

'He doesn't know we've moved here then?'

'Obviously not. Professor Babbage sounds a bit like our "esteemed friend" below, doesn't he? But Viv's piano's going to be delivered to the old flat today. We'll have to do something.'

'I suppose we could ring Viv?' Rachel suggested, feeling rather confused. 'How typical of him. They are a mad lot.'

'Marvellous to have a street piano. Tatiana can be the monkey on top.'

'I thought that was barrel organs,' Rachel said, pleased to see his excitement, and not wanting to dampen his enthusiasm with her own doubts.

'They had monkeys on them, yes, usually Italian ones, I think — players, not monkeys — but people used to muddle the barrel organs with these street pianos. Viv certainly wouldn't have muddled the terms. He knows what he's talking about.'

'Then this will be a piano?'

'A mechanically operated one. A pin and barrel one, worked by a handle.'

'I see, at least I will. But how big is it going to be?' Rachel knew Viv's optimism about squeezing in any number of instruments.

'Not sure. We'll see soon enough. I tell you what I think's the simplest. I'll go to the old flat and wait for it to arrive if it isn't already sitting in the hall!'

'And how will you get it out here? On your back, I suppose?' Rachel teased him.

'It'll be on wheels, I *think*. Then I'll see what can be done, see if the man will bring it on here. Or if I can, which is doubtful, by tube and train.'

'I suppose you could 'phone Viv first, and see if you could get in touch with the removal man beforehand.'

'Yes, then we might get it direct. I'll 'phone from up the road. You stay here, and, if I get no answer from Viv's, I'll go on to the old flat. All right?'

'Fine. I'll be gardening when I can,' Rachel said loudly, flashing her eyes at Matthias to warn him of their mother's return to the kitchen.

When they had all gone their separate ways, Rachel, left alone, tidied round vaguely then went on to the landing and looked down into the hall. The big house was absolutely quiet. No distant music floated up from an unseen source. She was not frightened by Bridge House as Tatiana was. Its age did not weigh down upon her in the same way, nor the strange and improbable stories which Tatiana repeated with complete belief. It must have been wonderful, Rachel thought, to be mistress of all this. It was odd the only wife of whom they knew, Amelia David, had not wanted to stay, even when she was a young bride. The house might have been fresh and beautiful then, tended by several maids, instead of one Miss Drube, and their own amateur efforts.

Rachel felt saddened. It seemed that Cousin Luke was willing to let the house die around him. He was merely using it as a protective shell, even against them. Yet she couldn't hate him with Tatiana's abandon, and just leave him locked away under cold grey skies.

CHAPTER EIGHT

M A T T H I A S seemed to be away a long time. Obviously, he had not been able to catch Viv. Rachel did not want to risk missing him by going out, even for a short time, and wandered through their part of the house, finally choosing to sit by a window overlooking the front gate with her herb catalogue.

It was an elegant black booklet describing the use and appearance of herbs, then their cultivation. The only disappointment was that March was too early for plants, even if she could afford them, and seeds would have to be planted in a greenhouse so early. April and May seemed to be the months when she might really make a start, put their roots into the soil she was now preparing. But would they be staying with Cousin Luke, putting down roots? Did his ignoring them mean any sort of acceptance?

Rachel sighed and turned back to make a list of what she would buy, if money were no object, just for her own satisfaction. If she chose by name it would be like a chant: 'Angelica, Balm, Basil, Coriander, Dill, Marjoram, Pennyroyal, Peppermint, Tansy.' But when she came to consider what she and her mother might use in their cooking, she had to admit that the chances of their making a dandelion stout, as recommended, with a Balm called *Melissa officinalis* were remote. She reminded herself to suggest to Matthias that they should make some as a present for Cousin Luke: the thought might appeal to Matthias. Meanwhile, what they definitely would use would be: Mint, Chives, Parsley, Sage and Common Thyme. The Lemon Thyme was a temptation, and she added it to her list with a question mark.

Rachel looked down into the garden. Already some daffodils were in bloom. It was an early Spring, but it would be silly to be so impatient that she wasted her money and lost plants to late frosts and fickle winds in the cold Spring days her mother called the Peewits' pinch. She wished she could remember the proper name for Adam's Candles, used as an old cure for toothache, to check if they were in the catalogue.

It was hard to know if they would be able to welcome the summer after this uncertain spring. Glancing down again, she saw that Cousin Luke was returning, enveloped in a long black macintosh, carrying a long black umbrella, looking, as Matthias had rudely said, like a 'skinny, limping old black crow'. Tatiana had danced round the kitchen singing, and limping with a ridiculous exaggeration till Mrs David stopped her. In fact, he did not limp, but, with his stick in one hand, and the umbrella held up in the other, looked remarkably vigorous for such an elderly man.

Rachel wished that she could understand him, but wondered if she ever would. She did not need to look at the clock to know that it was two o'clock, his regular time. She guessed that Matthias would have no time to think of lunch, nor spare money to buy any, so she went through to the kitchen, and occupied herself in making a pile of sandwiches, chutney and grated cheese, honey and date, to welcome him, and, she hoped, the street piano home.

Only a few minutes later, their door bell rang, and Rachel rushed down the back stairs.

Matthias was standing beside a large object, roughly covered with sheets of newspaper, secured with string.

'Help me in with it out of the rain. The bloke dropped me here as a favour, then had to dash off to catch up on another job, as he'd come out of his way. I said you'd help me with the rest.'

'Of course,' Rachel agreed, heaving gladly with him, pleased to see him after her long wait in the empty house.

They wheeled it into the corridor and shut the door. Matthias shook his wet hair and began to tear off the papers.

'It is quite big, isn't it?' Rachel commented as a squat looking upright piano shape on a wooden trolley came into view.

'A beauty, I think,' Matthias replied warmly, hanging his mac on the banister. 'Is Old Misery back?'

'Yes, he came in a few minutes ago. Why?'

'Just wondered. Looking at this and the stairs.'

Rachel glanced behind her at the old 'servants'' stairs and saw what he meant. The piano was about five feet high when on its base. They lifted it carefully off the four-wheeled trolley. It was about three and a half feet at its widest, heavy and bulky.

'Like a dumpy piano with a fat tummy,' she said.

'That's its barrel. You'll see.' Matthias patted the curved, black painted front.

Rachel peeked into the small mirror set in the upright front of the case between two country scenes in water colour. She read out the label.

'A. D. Lintle, M.A., King's Lynn, Norfolk.'

The top was attached by two leather straps at each side.

'Let's take the trolley up first,' Matthias suggested. 'I'm longing to *hear* it.'

They tipped the trolley on its side and Rachel went first, going hot as they edged round the bend in the stairs. By the time the trolley was on the first floor it was perfectly clear that it would be impossible to get the piano up that way.

'It will have to be up his stairs,' Matthias said. 'There really is no reason why he should mind. And the best thing, of course, is to see that he doesn't know. What the eye doesn't see, the heart doesn't grieve over. . . .'

'We could, of course, ask his permission,' Rachel said.

'*You* could, you mean. I'm not.'

'Well, I . . .' Rachel looked as dubious as she felt.

'On second thoughts, you can't. I'm not risking it. If he said "No", you'd feel obliged to obey, and I *am* getting it in, which I can't do alone. So you must help me. Please. It won't hurt him.'

'Agreed.' Rachel decided to swallow her doubts. 'He made such a fuss about *our* pictures being broken the day we came here, I couldn't bear that fuss again. We'll just have to creep across the hall in one go, so that there is no dull thud!'

Matthias laughed. 'If you let it go hard I bet there'd be a thud and twanging that would make his hair stand on end.'

'There's plenty in this house already,' Rachel answered, thinking of Tatiana's spectral music. 'Come on, before I lose my nerve.'

The piano was tremendously heavy. Rachel felt pain shoot in her aching arms. Somehow she lasted out to the bottom of the stairs. She stood there, her shoulders bursting. The stairs looked so big. They were wide, but there seemed so many of them.

Matthias looked at her appealingly. 'We'll stop at the top of the first flight for a breather. I'll make *you* some coffee if you get to the top.'

'If I live that long! All right. But will you nurse me if I dislocate my arms?'

They went up slowly. Matthias came behind, and was taking most of the weight, Rachel realised, as she saw his forehead running with perspiration. He was gritting his teeth and they were both panting at the top of the first flight, when they heard a sound from downstairs in the quiet house. A door had opened on to the hall below.

It would have been funny if she had not been so alarmed, Rachel realised. She was standing with Matthias at the top of the first flight of stairs, her back to the black velvet curtain, while they took a rest before attempting the last lap to their own landing. For no good reason she felt ridiculously guilty, flushed as if she were a five-year-old caught taking biscuits from the biscuit tin.

They stood stock still, foolishly holding on to the instrument, as if otherwise it would roll downstairs and land in a heap at his feet. Rachel was grateful to have something to hold as the stick tapped across the hall and Cousin Luke began to ascend the stairs with amazing agility.

His face was set, and he did not speak until he reached them, just looked through and beyond them to the black curtain.

'Why are you on these stairs? What are you doing? They are to be left alone. I made it perfectly clear. . . .'

'We're sorry, Cousin Luke. We'd have asked you if we'd have known. . . .' Rachel flinched before the unconcealed fury in his icy grey eyes and Matthias tried to help her out.

'You see sir, we've been given a present, and we couldn't get it up our stairs. We were afraid of damaging it. Or your paintwork,' he added with a slight grin, which soon faded. 'I mean we just thought it wouldn't disturb you if we brought it up this way.'

Cousin Luke towered over them both, looking with distaste at the tatty newspaper covering.

'It does trouble me exceedingly. I do not wish these stairs to be used by you as a thoroughfare, or indeed in any capacity. I shall speak to your mother.'

He narrowed his eyes and looked behind Rachel, who felt that it was up to her to break the stalemate. She could sense that Matthias was becoming angry, as one hand was tapping irritably on the instrument, and that wouldn't help.

'Please, don't bother my mother about this. You see, it's meant to be a present for *her*, and it would rather spoil it if it caused trouble, wouldn't it? We are sorry we've disturbed you.'

Matthias fidgeted beside her as the old man stared coldly at them in silence, so Rachel plunged on desperately:

'It's a mechanical instrument, you see. Some friends of

70

ours who're mad on instruments found two, and gave us, I mean her, one of them. I don't think it will make a great deal of noise though,' she added hastily, and with little private conviction. 'It may not be in proper working order,' she went on lamely.

Cousin Luke spoke at last. 'Show me.'

Rachel pulled off the newspapers with shaking fingers. Why was he so worked up about his precious stairs? They weren't as special as all that. Perhaps he was a little touched in the head, as Matthias maintained when they were together. He had the power to frighten her, so she could understand why Matthias stood there resentfully still, unable to risk offending 'Luke, our Landlord', as he called him behind his back.

Cousin Luke stood leaning on his stick looking intently at the instrument. He leaned towards it to see if there was a maker's name visible, and read the label.

'Take it upstairs and do not come here again.'

He turned and walked carefully downstairs, leaving them gaping.

Matthias raised his black eyebrows, then, scowling, turned his back on the old man and signalled Rachel to lift. They took the instrument straight upstairs and into Tatiana's bedroom. Now they were galvanised by a combination of relief and annoyance so, by unspoken agreement, they went the whole way without another break.

They plonked the instrument down. Rachel flopped on to the bed.

Matthias exploded: 'The miserable old so-and-so. He'll be putting burglar alarms on his perishing stairs next. Or trip ropes to catch the unwary. Anybody'd think they were solid gold. Or that we had a stuffed boa-constrictor or live skunk we were trying to smuggle in. Viv wouldn't believe it if I told him. I suppose it will make a good story sometime, when we get away from here, but at the moment it's pretty futile.'

'Never mind; we've got it in and up,' Rachel said comfortingly. 'And that's more than I expected when he charged up the stairs at us. I'd no idea he could move so fast.'

'What we used to call "Temper, temper".' Matthias smiled, his own good temper slightly restored. 'I rather thought he was going to set about it and reduce it to firewood for a few uncomfortable minutes.'

'Me too. He's easier to face sitting down. We're at such a disadvantage with him looming over us like that.'

Matthias was looking at the piano.

'You know,' Rachel said.

'Um. What?'

'He wasn't really angry.'

'Who?'

'Cousin Luke.'

Matthias did not answer, and Rachel went on: 'It was something else. Do you know what I think it was? When he saw the piano? He was *curious.*'

'What if he was.' Matthias was not interested. 'Perhaps none of his wartime lodgers heaved musical instruments upstairs. And I can see their point! I think that this handle might need a little oil. Just a drop.'

'Now I come to think of it, I'm sure he was dying for you to show it to him properly.'

'Doubt it. The old misery was only checking that we didn't scrape the hideous brown paint on his precious staircase. I don't know why you're so interested all the time in what *he* thinks. I'm not. The main thing now we've got it here is to get it working for Mummy and . . .'

He broke off and produced a loud deliberate jangle as he adjusted the instrument.

Rachel did not need to be told that he had nearly mentioned their father, who would have loved this extravagant and unexpected present.

She went and made coffee for both of them and said no more to Matthias about Cousin Luke, though in her own mind she could not stop puzzling about him.

CHAPTER NINE

MATTHIAS had lifted up the top of the piano, then taken out the front panel. Rachel sat on the bed, clasping a cup of coffee between her hands, watching him.

He spoke quickly, excitedly: 'You see, it's a simple upright piano whose keyboard has been replaced by a long barrel. Here are the strings stretched vertically. The handle at the side rotates the barrel. Pins on the barrel make the hammers strike the strings, just as if someone were pressing the keys down with his fingers. It's the nineteenth-century version of the mechanically plucked spinet. But this would make a fine noise for street musicians, and no skill needed either; not like a hurdy-gurdy, or bagpipes.'

'Why *is* it such a noisy instrument compared with an ordinary upright piano?'

'Well, a hand player can make a piano note last by holding down the key. But the only way to sustain a single note in this thing was to repeat it quickly. That's why it jangles. It's rather good.'

He turned the handle on the front and the room was filled with brash jingling sound. Rachel hastily closed the door, but smiled at him.

'A treat for Cousin Luke's days out. It's like a fairground.'

'It's marvellous. In a crude way, it's music that no human player could make, and that fascinates me.'

'But you don't count it as real music, do you?' Rachel asked.

'Absolutely real,' Matthias answered, seriously. 'Some of the greatest composers wrote for mechanical organ clocks. Mozart, Schubert and Beethoven. And Beethoven liked mechanical pianos. These mechanical instruments gave enormous pleasure to ordinary people, who couldn't play instruments or read music, but the most intriguing thing for composers, I'm sure, was that, to a certain extent, they gave perfect performances.'

'How do you mean?'

'In a way, machines, if they're working well, give flaw-less performances, because they are less variable than human performers. No human interpreter stands between the composer's idea of his music and its playing by an instrument.'

'That's a bit complicated. I take your word for it. What is the other handle for, do you think?'

'To change the tune. It moves the barrel from left to right and right to left. It has ten tunes listed here. We know a lot of them: "Santa Lucia, Sunshine Waltz, Here, There and Everywhere, a March, Sing a Song of Sixpence."' He turned the handle and played through 'The Keel Row' but he no longer looked pleased and frowned into the instrument.

'In fact, that's what's exciting about electronic music. The composer can be his own interpreter completely. You see'; he spoke slowly, as if working it out for himself, 'he makes a composition in sounds. He can make electric vibrations, pure sounds like a tuning fork noise, or "square waves", which can be buzzing and hissing and all sorts. He can mix these up together by using several tape record-ers, and playing the sounds at different speeds. You know the sort of difference if you switch the record player to 78 for a long player which should be 33. It completely changes the music, weirdly.'

'Is that *musique concrète*?'

'No, *musique concrète* uses ordinary sounds, from traditional instruments, noises from bottles, jugs, anything, records them, then manipulates *those* sounds to make music, speeding and slowing up tapes. They call them *objets sonores*, sounding objects. But I don't think there's much distinction now between electronic and concrete music, except by theorists arguing at experimental festivals. It's just, I suppose, synthetic music, by electronic means, from instruments and objects.'

'But *is* that music?' Rachel objected. 'The sort of stuff I mean sounds like wireless atmospherics, or the sound track for frightening films, or television background for space flight.'

'It is good for the fantastic, I know, but I think it can be music. It's better not to think of traditional music at all, but let this speak for itself differently: sound organised into an appreciable pattern, but a new one.'

'But if you are quite content with the old patterns. . . . Why make such an effort?'

'I suppose for the sake of exploration. Because the mountain is there, the climbers climb. Because we want to go beyond the sounds of man-made instruments and see what is there.'

'So far, all I've heard is very limited. Just bitty and boring. Not lovely to hear, but ugly. No shape and inhuman. Yes, that's it. I think it frightens me, even without men from Mars glaring from the screen as well.'

'I know what you mean. But that's quite a strong response to the sounds. And, of course, some composers have mixed in human voices. Stockhausen has, for instance.'

Rachel wrinkled up her nose.

'Give me a practised pianist or a humble street piano any day.'

He patted the instrument. 'I'm not saying anything against this. And after all, this was the Victorians' equivalent of a tape recorder or gramophone.'

'I must say it couldn't be tossed about like those marvellous new record players which even work upside down,' Rachel said, ruefully rubbing her sore shoulders. 'I vow I'll never move *this* "sound object" another inch. When we leave here the removal men have my sympathy.'

'They'll need danger money to pass those stairs!'

'By the way, don't mention that scene to Tatiana. She gets worked up enough about the old man. And it'll only worry Mummy.'

'All right.' He sighed. 'It is fascinating though.'

'What? His mania about a flight of stairs?'

'No. Not that. The production of sounds. I was going to do so much.'

'You mean electronic composition?'

'No. You'd need buckets of money for that — a generator for producing pure sounds, at least three tape recorders, yards of tape which costs the earth anyhow, amplifiers, filters, heaven knows what else.' He hesitated, then went on with an effort: 'I, we were going to do some experiments, Daddy and I, with his voice and other recorded sounds. He was going to be the musician and me the engineer. You remember he borrowed that Transirecorder? We were going to try things out with that. This mechanical monster we've lugged up here reminded me of my own mechanical leanings, that's all. Only this is working quite well, doesn't need much engineering. And I've lost the heart.'

'Perhaps Viv sent it deliberately to you as well as Mummy,' Rachel suggested. 'Did he know about this idea? I never realised you were doing more than recording things you liked and trying to improve your own tape recorder, and quality of production.'

77

'It hadn't got much further than that. There wasn't any room in the flat.'

Matthias turned away abruptly, and, before she could answer, again filled the room with exuberant, vibrant strumming. Suddenly, the door was opened. For a panicky moment, Rachel expected to see an infuriated Cousin Luke.

But it was Tatiana who stood in the doorway, astounded then delighted. She kicked off her shoes, started to move to the music, irresistibly keeping time. She stalked round the room, bending her legs into an angle at the knee, then stretching them out fully with the toes pointed in a long straight line, her hands stuck out comically behind as a small tail.

'What is it? A barrel organ piano?'

'Perhaps you mean a street gurdy!' Matthias laughed at her as she peered into the instrument on tip toe.

'It's a mechanical instrument, playing recognisable tunes. I can tell you that.' Rachel said. 'People call them piano organs and all sorts of names, but Matthias calls it a street piano.'

'Is it ours then?'

'No, it's really a present for Mummy, from Viv. Only we got it up here secretly, while she was out. So don't go and blab.'

'Course I won't. It's a mechanical piano, is it? Stravinsky was going to use one for *Les Noces* at first. That *and* an electric harmonium, two cymbaloms and percussion. Miss Julian told me when she went to see it. Diaghilev burst into tears when he heard it. Miss Julian told me.'

'Then it must be true,' said Matthias.

'What instruments did Stravinsky use in the end?' Rachel put in the question hastily.

'Four pianos with percussion. Don't you remember? I told you. And a chorus too.'

'I only remember about the dancing, how you said you'd like to be the Bride one day, you with your long plaits.'

'Pigtails,' Matthias said, flicking one by its yellow ribbon. 'By the time Tatiana's a prima ballerina she may be dancing to electronic music, not Tchaikovsky or Stravinsky.'

'You mean yours?' Rachel asked, thinking she might spur him on.

'Oh, I'm just curious, but some has already been tried for ballet.'

Tatiana pulled a face at him and said: 'I bet it would sound peculiar. But don't you want to hear my news?'

'What's that? The Royal Ballet can't manage a day longer without you?'

'I shan't tell if you're rude.'

'I bet there's nothing to tell.' Matthias was testing a piano string with his finger, tightening the little peg holding it with a clock key he had produced.

'I've learnt some more about Amelia.'

'Who on earth's Amelia? Miss Drube?'

'No. Cousin Luke's wife, Amelia,' Rachel explained.

'You knew her name?' Tatiana pouted slightly.

'Yes, you told me before, but what else did you find out?' Rachel was genuinely interested, and Matthias was actually listening too.

'She did not exactly leave him. They had a quarrel, and she ran away. It was about something in the house he wouldn't get rid of. It was . . .'

'I know. The *front staircase*!' Matthias interrupted before Rachel's warning glance could stop him.

Tatiana was furious, her dramatic moment spoilt.

'All right then, I won't tell you,' she cried. 'I'll go and look at it for myself. *And* I shan't tell you what I find.'

She flounced out of the room, flinging the door hard so that it slammed noisily.

Rachel winced. 'This house is big enough, but it needs sound-proofing for her temperament at times. You did spoil it a bit for her, her big moment.'

'Oh, she makes everything so momentous, it's a bore. And I expect this is just something Miss Drube's made up to please her.'

'Never mind. We'll have tea soon. That'll cheer her up. I'll go and ask her about the London Museum.'

'The original good audience. Except, may I say, for electronic music!'

CHAPTER TEN

MRS DAVID was back in time for tea, and hardly noticed their request to keep away from the secret in Tatiana's room, because she was so excited herself.

'Rachel, tea all ready! How lovely! I'm so thirsty too, because we didn't seem to stop talking the whole time I was there. It turned into a real party. I'll tell you about it. Can you put this on a plate? A share for you of my treat.'

Even Tatiana cheered up a little when she saw the ice-cream gâteau her mother had brought back for tea. Rachel divided it up quickly, determined that her mother's delight should not be marred by any account of the latest row between Matthias and Tatiana.

'First of all, Tim sent his love to you three, and said he'd send us some tickets for the next production.'

Mrs David picked up her tea cup and put it down again without tasting the tea. Her face was alive and softened with excitement; her eyes seemed brighter, and Rachel remembered how pretty her mother could look, when she was happy.

'It turned into a party because *the* Italian visitor was Giuseppe Marcello.'

'The conductor?'

'Yes, you remember Daddy met him in Milan, and raved about him. He's the one they call Wonder Boy over here.'

'Why?' Tatiana asked. 'Is he a *boy* like Matthias?'

Mrs David didn't notice the attempted scorn.

'Not really, but he's very young to have achieved what he has. He's immensely talented. He won a conducting competition over here, and conducted at the Festival Hall not so long ago, but I think his heart is in opera. He trained for a while as a singer, and certainly knows a lot about it. I believe he makes his orchestras "sing", and he's famous for persuading the strings to produce that superb warm tone they can. And he has a beautiful speaking voice, rather soft, quite an accent left, but good English.'

'Is he going to be a visiting conductor or to produce opera, or what?' Rachel asked.

'He *is* going to produce his first operas over here, though he's done quite a bit over in Italy, I believe, conducting and producing and so on.'

'Then how old is he?'

'It's hard to say. Under thirty, I should think. He has black hair, but a few white hairs over his ears — you know the sort of thing.'

'Distinguished, but too old for you,' Matthias teased Rachel. 'So Tim coughed up a tremendous lunch to give Giuseppe Marcello a false idea of what he'll really get when he comes to work here.'

'He's come! He's here for some weeks. And I've heard that once he's in rehearsal he forgets time, and unimportant things like meals.'

'Poor singers and players,' commented Tatiana, regretfully finishing her portion of gâteau. 'He won't be very popular if he gives them no breaks, will he?'

'They may not all have wolfish appetites. Some people live for their "Art",' Matthias said meaningfully.

'I think he'll manage them all right,' Mrs David said. 'He could charm the birds off the tree. In fact . . .' she hesitated, 'he's rather talked me into doing something for him.'

'What?' Rachel asked.

'He's persuaded me to act as *répétiteur* for several Master Classes he's taking. The pianist who was to have worked with him has injured his wrist. When I arrived, Tim drew me into his office, and said they'd had a terrible crisis, 'phoning round, trying to find someone at the last minute who was really competent to work with Marcello. He's a terrible perfectionist, I imagine, and drives the pianists hard, expecting them to be "with" him the whole time.'

'What would you do then?' Tatiana asked. 'Accompany the lesson?'

'Yes, that sort of thing. You see, I said I wasn't really in practice, but if they were works I knew, I'd be willing to have a try. I have done a lot of it from a piano score so often with your father, that sort of thing is familiar to me. Tim waved all my objections aside, saying I was just being a modest violet.'

'And you'd love to have a chance to do it,' Rachel added.

'I would, though no doubt I'll have terrible misgivings when I actually face this demanding young man as his *répétiteur*, rather than as a fellow guest at a gorgeous lunch.'

'He ought to be grateful to you,' Matthias said loyally, 'stepping in at the last moment.'

'It is rather late in the day. That's why it was so hard to find anyone else. Tim was delighted, almost fell on my neck when I said I'd have a try, because the Class is partly in a way an audition too. They have further plans for next season, and, of course, they're always on the lookout for promising students.'

'It's a Class for students? Well, *they* won't notice any wrong notes,' Rachel said practically.

'But I will, and I bet Giuseppe Marcello will too! Some students and some professionals, I think it will be. It was all arranged in such a rush. Tim wanted to 'phone me this evening to tell me more, and I had to explain that Cousin Luke didn't run to new-fangled twentieth-century telephones. But I *shall* ring him up from the call box. I left them deep in discussions, and came home with the piano scores of *Figaro* and *Rigoletto*, the editions he wants to use.'

'And a luscious gâteau. You can go up any day you bring one of these home,' Tatiana told her mother. 'I had a lovely time with Miss Drube too. She's quite fun, and *we* had a good lunch too.'

'You missed the rain? I seemed to dodge the worst of the showers.'

Mrs David at last started to drink her tea.

'You deserve some sunshine,' Rachel said softly to herself.

*　　*　　*

It turned into a cold wet evening, and they were all glad to be indoors in what they used to call the 'warmey'. Rachel, looking down into the garden, felt that Spring was dragging its feet; she wanted to see what Summer would bring. Matthias had drifted off upstairs to his room, after a private gloat over the street piano. Tatiana, her rage forgotten, sat curled up in an armchair, oblivious of the world, reading the life story of her favourite ballerina.

Rachel settled on a cushion leaning against a leg of the piano, content to dream as her mother played from the scores to refresh her memory. She did not look sad, only serious, concentrating hard, but Rachel clenched her idle hands as she caught herself waiting for her father's voice, for Rigoletto to sing to his belovéd daughter, Gilda.

Mrs David skipped through the opera, picking out the main arias, then turned to the third act of *The Marriage*

84

of Figaro, practising the intricate accompaniments until she was satisfied that they rippled with ease. From the third act she played the March for the wedding procession, flourishing the repeated notes for her own enjoyment. She broke off to remind Tatiana of bedtime and to say good night, and otherwise was completely lost in the music when Rachel sleepily followed, not long afterwards.

She fell asleep quickly, but was woken by shaking from a heavy slumber, which made her dazed and confused when she saw Tatiana, her long hair falling over her shoulders, pale and urgent.

'Wake up, Rachel. Wake up. I'm so frightened. You must wake up.'

'I am awake,' Rachel answered, partly to convince herself that she would become fully conscious and drag herself from the depths if given time.

Tatiana was sitting on the bed shivering, staring at her fixedly. Rachel sat up, propping herself on one elbow.

'Now what is it?' she asked soothingly. 'Anybody'd think the house was falling down. And where's your dressing-gown?'

'I forgot it.'

'Put mine on. You're freezing, you silly.'

'I'm frightened,' Tatiana repeated. 'Rachel, that music. I heard it again.'

'It'll be Mummy practising, that's all. She was still at it when I came to bed.'

'It wasn't. The drawing-room was dark, and her door shut to. I came up to you because I'd told you about it, and I was too scared on my own.'

'There's nothing to be scared about,' Rachel said. 'Honestly, for a dancer to be frightened by music is ridiculous. And I expect it was Matthias, if not Mummy. He often tries things over late at night. At the moment, I can't hear anything.'

They both sat still. The only sound was of wind, and rain blowing against window panes. Then Tatiana clutched Rachel's arm.

'There it is. You see, I wasn't making it up.'

There was a sound of faint music. It seemed to come from a great distance, far further away than Matthias' room next door, Rachel realised at once. She strained her ears to recognise the tune, to make it ordinary. But it came merely as a high, unearthly tinkle, and she switched on the light, for her own benefit as well as Tatiana's.

'Yes, I did hear something that time,' she admitted. 'And it was some sort of music.'

'Ghosts,' Tatiana announced dramatically. 'I'm sure this house is haunted.'

'I don't see why,' Rachel maintained stoutly, pushing on

slippers and pulling on a sweater. 'Come and investigate.'

'No thank you!' Tatiana had crept into the vacant place in Rachel's bed. 'You can have your dressing-gown. I'll wait here with the light on. You are brave to go. What if you meet something? Or someone?'

'I don't believe in that sort of Thing or Person,' Rachel answered, 'and I expect there's a perfectly reasonable explanation for it all. Cousin Luke . . .'

'Hasn't got a wireless, or a record player, or a television or a piano. Miss Drube told me. And she goes to bed early,' Tatiana said triumphantly. 'You see; it's something super — what's the word, superactual.'

'Supernatural. I don't think so for a moment. I'll go and investigate since you've woken me up thoroughly now. And I'll start by checking on Matthias. You stay here then?'

'I shan't move. Don't worry. And if Anything comes for me, I'll shriek for Matthias.'

'He would be surprised and flattered,' Rachel commented wryly, as she tightened her dressing-gown belt and went out on to the landing.

From there, she could faintly hear the tinkling music, but it definitely was not from Matthias' room. No light showed beneath his door, and she resisted the temptation to wake him for support, turned instead down the stairs to the next landing. There again she paused and listened. The music was a little clearer and surely came from below. It was eerie, she had to admit. But it was real. She nerved herself to go on.

As Tatiana had reported, the drawing-room and her mother's room were dark. Straining her ears in darkness seemed to make her hear more acutely: she did not want to wake her mother, whose door was now a little ajar, by switching on the landing light. Yet Rachel, in spite of her good sense, trembled a little, and not with cold, as she walked towards the prohibited main staircase. Having come so far, she was not going to retreat without satisfaction for practical sense, and reassurance for her fearful young sister.

She stole down the stairs, guiding herself by a hand on the banisters, determined not to notice that it shook slightly as the music went on in the dimly glowing ground floor. When she reached the hall, she saw that in the back corner the door of Cousin Luke's secret room was open. She had worked out before that this must be the way in to his private room, the one with shuttered windows. And now the light was on, and the music coming from within, surely from a music box!

It was playing 'Daisy Bell', slowing down so that the jangles became separated into drawls of notes. Rachel felt impelled to cross the hall, and discover the centre of the mystery. She walked as if still in her dreams, the words playing through her head:

> Daisy, Daisy, give me your answer, do!
> I'm half crazy all for the love of you.
> It won't be a stylish marriage.
> I can't afford a carriage.
> But you'll look sweet
> Upon the seat
> Of a bicycle made for two.

She had reached the open door. Cousin Luke was sitting at a table, rigidly upright. But his head sagged forward on to his chest. The music came to a stop, unwillingly, it seemed, releasing the last notes from their wooden prison.

Rachel stepped down the two steps impulsively, struck with a disturbing thought: Cousin Luke sat so still.

'Was he dead?'

CHAPTER ELEVEN

As soon as she reached him, Rachel realised at once that he was merely asleep, breathing shallowly, and so she dared to look round the room.

Now she was within, it was difficult to decide what she had expected, but this was a surprise. For the room was somehow not his, although he spent so much time there. It was small and soft and pink. That was it, a feminine room. Even as the thought came to her mind Rachel looked up at a portrait of a young woman, sitting on a curved white stool, loosely holding some common daisies and London Pride in small hands. Her blonde hair was drawn loosely back from a centre parting. Rachel stared at the deep rose pink dress, with a sailor collar and bow, the large pearl buttons through the dress. It was a young style. Perhaps she was only a young girl then, for Rachel knew who gazed down upon her, half smiling. It was Amelia.

Of course, she had married her own cousin young, and perhaps she was then eighteen or so, and years younger than Cousin Luke. Rachel could understand why Mr Murdoch had found her pretty. She looked so fresh and youthful, just as he said, like an English rose. Perhaps Tatiana might look like that one day. Rachel stared again. In fact, they were, in a way, alike. Tatiana had the same corn gold hair and blue eyes. After all, Amelia would be their cousin too. Did she ever remind Cousin Luke of this frozen youth of his young wife, who had never returned?

Perhaps that was why he was so hostile towards Tatiana. Was that possible? Or was the dead silence of the room oppressing her, frightening her into wild fancies?

Rachel looked away from the portrait, at the music box on a small round piecrust table. It was an oblong box in varnished brown wood, inlaid with a leaf pattern in paler woods. The lid was open and a faded card decorated with a player and his lady, birds and blossom, gave a list of the ten tunes, written in curly writing with a dip pen, the red ink faded. Rachel could see 'Genève' printed in one corner, then read:

> Daisy Bell . Dacre.
> My Old Dutch . Incles.
> Molly and I and the Baby . Kennedy.

She did not read them all. The box itself was in three compartments, two smaller ones on either side of the central, glass covered part, where the metal barrel, covered with tiny pins, would revolve slowly against a metal comb with graded teeth. A cog wheel to the left was joined to the brass winding handle in one side partition. The other had two small levers, marked Change, Repeat and Stop, Play.

Rachel glanced back at the picture. There again was the same table, and the same box, beside Amelia. Perhaps it was a present to her. The whole room was dominated by the full length portrait which nearly filled one wall. In effect, the room was still Amelia's, Rachel realised, as she now noticed a crusty silver-backed hair brush and hand mirror, side by side. The silver was dented and old looking, but lovingly polished, she presumed on Miss Drube's grudgingly permitted cleaning visits, like the one she had overheard. The bristles were yellowed. They had brushed

no hair, she assumed, for all these years. And no lady had sat in the little pink velvet armchair. The shutters were closed, and the rose pink curtains drawn back. Perhaps if they were moved too much they would crumble away, Rachel thought, by now convinced that the room had been kept untouched, unchanged ever since Amelia ran away.

She looked back on Cousin Luke sitting in this dead, preserved room, perhaps with a ghost for company. That seemed possible in a room where the clock had stopped or even been made to stop. But it was not the sort of ghost to frighten, not even Tatiana. She could only imagine that this was Amelia's own little withdrawing-room, her boudoir, and that he had kept it exactly the same, all these years, in case she should return.

Yet she never had returned. Rachel shifted on her feet and considered the young woman who never had grown old, or not in this house beside Cousin Luke. In sleep, he appeared pathetically old, with wrinkled eyelids, not the hard-eyed guardian of his privacy who so alarmed Tatiana. His thin mouth was relaxed, almost into a smile, and Rachel wondered if he, now so frail, was dreaming of a vigorous youth. When awake, he seemed so much less vulnerable. Then he was in command, but now defenceless, caught unawares.

She turned to creep away. It would be appalling to be caught intruding, eavesdropping almost on his conversation with the past. Her cheeks flushed at the thought of his waking suddenly, but he did not stir as she moved back towards the door. His stillness emboldened her to pause by a large leather album with metal clasps, on a low table. It was propped open, and she could read on the corner of the first page, in Cousin Luke's black handwriting:

For Amelia, in restitution, a history of Bridge House until it died, the day she went away. By the caretaker until he dies, in 19..., Luke David.

'How extraordinary,' thought Rachel, gazing at the thick pages covered with close writing, sometimes broken by old prints, a small oil painting, all of the house, the garden and the river. A collection of dim browny photographs was arranged alongside, to be included later, she supposed. 'He's done all this for her, and she will, I suppose, never read it.' Rachel shuddered. It was so strangely forlorn, all this careful labour, a huge album to be filled with his work. He did not intend to publish the history of the house, she assumed, merely to record it for Amelia, who, for her own reasons, had not cared enough to stay there.

He was not fierce now, not to be hated, Rachel decided, creeping away, but oddly to be pitied.

She found Tatiana fast asleep in her bed, and so went downstairs to Tatiana's room for the rest of the night. First she wrote a note: 'You were asleep when I came back. NO GHOSTS. Just a music box, left on by Cousin Luke. See you in the morning. Rachel.'

Yet when she lay in Tatiana's bed, although she was now warm again and comfortable, Rachel could not sleep. She thought of the old man downstairs, deliberately isolated from them all, and so alone. She could not 'give away' what she had found out only by chance and curiosity, but it did make her determined to do what she could to reach him in some way, without shattering his privacy or hurting his pride.

*   *   *

When Rachel awoke the next morning, snowflakes were blowing wildly against a thick grey sky. Huge flakes were white on the sprouting brilliant green and yellow, tawny new rose leaves. Some forsythia was full out, and daffodils. Gusts of wind blew the snow, then let it drift down steadily. No white carpet settled on the wet ground and the sky changed cloudily; the snow became sleet as Rachel watched, fascinated.

In this house by the river, she was more conscious of the weather this freakish Spring, when so much else was doubtful. She remembered one cold Sunday morning, when the river lay invisible behind a curtain of mist. She had gone down to the water and mist floated on the surface in the cold air. Then a yellow disc of sun had appeared in the sky

93

at half past ten, and broke through to flawless skies and a mild mellow afternoon.

Did Cousin Luke, she reflected, ever wonder how many more times he would look out to the new start of Spring? Did he care?

The sleet was now rain, but the steady breeze might blow it away and free her for the garden.

'Hello. Have you been changing rooms?'

Mrs David had come into the room, and Rachel turned round.

'Tatiana had a bit of a nightmare. She heard sounds in the house. She came up to my room, and I came down to check up, then she had fallen asleep, so I pinched her bed.'

'I see,' Mrs David was listening in a preoccupied way, not bothered at all. Rachel realised that she was excited.

'What time does the Master Class begin?'

'Ten. You're sure you'll be all right? It looks a foul day. Can you manage a hot lunch for the others? They'll need it. I shan't be back till late afternoon, I should guess. If this rain goes on, you might all go to the cinema. See what you think.'

'Don't worry. We'll be all right. There's plenty here. I can give them a choice of menu, while you'll be slaving away at the piano, lucky if he lets you off for five minutes to eat a sandwich.'

Mrs David laughed. 'I shan't mind, for one day. Perhaps he relaxes sometimes. He might like to come out here. I know he's keen on recording techniques, so Matthias would enjoy meeting him. Now we're more or less settled, we could have some friends out.'

'More or less. I suppose we have done quite well.' Rachel tried to be encouraging. 'Shall I go and wake the others?'

'We'll give them a shout when breakfast's ready. I'm in

such a good mood today they can crawl down in dressing gowns if they like.'

*　　*　　*

Matthias and Tatiana dawdled so long over breakfast, having a toast-eating competition, that Rachel thought that they wouldn't be able to eat much lunch when the time came.

Mrs David set off with the *Figaro* score, having only managed to drink coffee. Somehow, her excitement had communicated itself, and Matthias said:

'It's one of the old man's mornings out, isn't it?'

'Yes it is, though I didn't see him go,' Rachel answered.

'Too busy eating toast but pretending not to be as piggish as us! You'll be buying binoculars next, or lace curtains so you can peer down at him, tracking his movements without being seen! I can't see how you find him so irresistibly interesting.'

Rachel didn't mind this good-natured teasing, though she was not going to be drawn. 'Why don't we try out the street piano?' she suggested, 'while Mummy's out, and him too.'

'Good idea, and there's something else I'd like to try while we've got a bit of peace.'

'A chance to disturb the peace, you mean. Is it something highly electronic?' Rachel asked.

'No, really very trad. music this time. Just your low level,' Matthias answered. 'You wait. One day, I'll persuade you there is some music in the other stuff too.'

'I doubt it.'

'I think there's rhythm and pattern in some electronic music.' Tatiana unexpectedly supported Matthias. 'And that makes it music for a dancer, you know.'

'I do know,' Matthias agreed. 'Some of the new ballet scores are very adventurous. I read about one the other day for bugle, voice, percussion and some odd instrument called the Bronte.'

'Played by human beings presumably, not machines though?' Rachel asked.

'You come and hear my machine,' Matthias said. 'I've got a stunning recording and I've been longing to play it full blast. You'll like it too.'

They all three went up to Matthias' room and he picked out a record and put it on the record player. 'Really traditional, I promise.'

The record revolved slowly and drums started to roll and beat. Then children began to sing with an enjoyable stridency:

> This old man, he played one,
> He played nick-nack on my drum.
> Nick-nack, paddy-wack, give a dog a bone,
> This old man came rolling home.

Instruments joined in gradually as the numbers mounted. Tatiana laughed with wicked delight and joined in the singing, then began to dance. A piccolo now played the tune and the drums beat unceasingly to a tremendous climax with the other instruments before they faded away into the distance.

'Again, while our old man is out,' pleaded Tatiana, who had contrived to fit a minute polka step to the exuberant march, her hands crossed loosely behind her back.

'With pleasure, Miss Fonteyn.' Matthias bowed. 'Let me turn the music a little louder. Just listen to that bass. I've got it on tape too.' He flung open the door and put on a tape this time.

'Five, four, three, two, one. Blast off!'

Certainly it was full blast. The house seemed to be saturated with sound. Rachel laughingly backed out into the corridor, her hands over her ears. Tatiana now did huge skips with straightening legs, shaping with her arms a curving drum round and round in front of her body. She danced ecstatically, as if the music changed her arms to wings, and her taut feet could impel her flight. She had already reached David's landing. Rachel half imagined that she would not need to touch the stairs as she stepped on still further downwards: she stepped and pointed, each leg in turn arching out and away. A hand glided down the banister as she touched it lightly for balance. The drums pulsed into their ears. The bass throbbed beneath and Tatiana went on below.

'Not loud enough?' Matthias shouted, and turned the sound up to full extent.

Rachel leaned over to watch Tatiana. Gradually the drums were retreating. Then suddenly repeated screams came echoing up to them, shocking after the joyous music.

Rachel almost fell down the first flight of stairs, then down again to the next landing, sick with terror.

CHAPTER TWELVE

TATIANA was standing by the black curtain, drawn back and showing a glint of mirror behind her clutching hands, which held the curtain as if she needed that support to prevent her from cowering on the floor in front of Cousin Luke. For she was abject with fear.

As she ran towards them, Rachel saw Cousin Luke shaking Tatiana by the shoulder:

'You've looked there. You've moved the curtain. You wicked disobedient child! How did you know what was there? I told you all to keep away from these stairs. And you, most of all. . . .'

'Cousin Luke.' Rachel forced herself into the appalling scene.

He turned on her, white with anger. 'I thought that you were a sensible girl, and yet you permitted this outrage.'

His shaking hand fell from Tatiana's shoulder and she stood gulping, half sobbing, but in a smothered way, as if fearful to attract any more attention.

Rachel was bewildered by this sudden shattering of their happy mood, and spoke slowly, choosing words with care as she tried to work out why he was so beside himself.

'We didn't mean any harm, I promise you. We thought you were out, or we'd never have played such loud music. We didn't mean to disturb you.'

'Disturb me! Your young sister has disturbed more than me. This is no ordinary house. Or staircase.'

'We know you like it private, and we're sorry to have trespassed. I'm sure Tatiana is,' Rachel glanced at her promptingly, then ploughed on desperately into the ominous silence. 'You see, she was just dancing, and got carried away. Didn't you, Tatiana?'

'But why move the curtain?' Cousin Luke demanded, glaring down at Tatiana from his great height.

'I knew there was a mirror there. I was practising an "Attitude". We do it in class. We correct our posture that way. I used the banister as a sort of *barre*,' Tatiana mumbled to her motionless feet.

'How did you know?'

'I'd looked before. I . . .'

'But what is so terrible about looking in the mirror?'

Matthias had joined them, and Rachel was grateful, until he added:

'Why all the fuss?'

Cousin Luke answered with icy scorn. 'Even in mirrors there are things unseen. Even mirrors cannot reveal everything. And what is unseen is most to be feared. Your sister may come to know what I mean.'

Tatiana shrank against the black curtain.

Cousin Luke ignored her, and spoke to Rachel in an even voice. 'This time, I shall speak to your mother.'

'Oh please, Cousin Luke, don't worry her. This is our row, and our doing. She's had enough trouble, and she's been so grateful to you for letting us stay here. We won't ever come on your stairs again.'

'The damage is done, I believe,' Cousin Luke stated grimly. 'You chose to ignore my requests and warnings.'

'But,' Matthias exploded angrily. 'The kid's only looked in a mirror, for goodness sake.'

'Oh Matthias, don't . . .' Rachel said, but he put his arm protectively round Tatiana's shoulder, drew her away from the curtain and went on defiantly: 'We don't know why you let us come and live here, if you cannot bear the sight of us — in your precious mirror, or otherwise.'

'I was persuaded,' Cousin Luke said bleakly. 'And indubitably it was an error of judgement, which I regret. Go back to your rooms. I shall speak to your mother.'

Rachel pushed them upwards. 'Don't say any more,' she urged. 'Leave it for now.'

They trailed upstairs, conscious of his staring eyes, all the way. It was a relief to get into the kitchen and shut the door. Tatiana sat on a chair and wept, not with her usual noisy enjoyment after a scene, but quietly and hopelessly, with her arms cradling her head on the table. Rachel heard her whisper 'Why did Daddy have to die?' and ached with misery, which turned to resentment against Cousin Luke.

'What can we do now?' Matthias asked. 'Never mind the old man. He's an old devil.'

'I don't understand it,' Rachel said. 'What is it about those stairs, that mirror?'

'Oh, he's ravers.'

'Sssh. Don't say that. You'll frighten her more,' Rachel whispered, and came to a decision. 'I don't think he is at all. He's just obsessed by the house.' She remembered fleetingly the painstaking History she had seen, the old man asleep in the dead room. Even now, she could not exactly hate him; at this distance, at least, she was not so much afraid as disturbed, and still, unremittingly, curious. She had to find out, but, for the moment, it was more urgent to make their peace, somehow. Surely, he needed it too. She sensed that he was apprehensive about what lay behind the curtain.

'Let him cool down a bit,' Rachel advised.

'Cool down! He's a perishing iceberg anyhow,' Matthias said, looking at Tatiana, hoping the insult would cheer her up, but she did not lift her head.

'I think that the best thing is for me to go and warn Mummy that we've had a spot of bother here. . . .'

'Understatement of the year.'

'And you two could go out somewhere. Why don't you have a snack lunch at the coffee bar and go to that film at the Odeon? I've got some money you can have.'

'Get out of here for a while, you mean?'

'Yes,' and Rachel nodded meaningly at Tatiana.

'What will you do? Go to the Master Class, drag her from the piano stool, then spill the beans?'

'No. I'll see if I can catch her for a word in a lull. It's not as far as the Opera House. They're in an old cinema, which is sometimes used for rehearsals — the old Roxy — only about half an hour away. You two go, and we'll have a big tea, say about half past five. All right?'

Matthias agreed and Rachel took Tatiana into the bath-room, and bathed her red eyelids with cold cotton wool, soothed her and talked to her until she was calm and quieter.

'He's just old and strange. I expect anyone would be if they'd lived on their own for so long in a great big house.'

'Miss Drube has been here too. And it's more than old age. I know. She's told me.'

'You mustn't take old *stories* so to heart,' Rachel chided her. 'You'll only upset yourself, don't you see?'

'I wish,' Tatiana replied positively, 'that we could leave here today, this afternoon, and never come back.'

'Well, we can't,' Rachel tried to be brisk, though she merely felt exhausted. 'And Mummy's had enough diffi-culties, without us *making* more. When we *can* get some-thing better, we will. So we must put up with this for now. And help her make it work. Promise me you'll try.'

'All right,' Tatiana agreed grudgingly. 'But if I could get away from here and live at a ballet school, I'd go tomorrow.'

'Don't say that to Mummy. I know what you mean. But you'll see. He'll simmer down. People do. Now you go off to the film, forget him for a while. He's just old and crotchety, that's all.'

*   *   *

On the way to the old Roxy, Rachel went through the whole scene again in her mind, trying to decide how to tell her mother what had happened with Cousin Luke. Was it just obstinacy that made him so stringent about his rules, or something more? He seemed so excessively worried about Tatiana's trespassing.

Rachel felt nervous, barging into the Master Class, and hoped that she'd be able to slip in quietly, unseen, so was relieved to find one of the old plate glass doors was ajar. As she passed the empty ticket kiosk she heard a piano playing. She pushed aside the velvet curtain, sharply reminded of Cousin Luke's black one, and sank quickly into the back row of the stalls, to take her bearings.

Only the cinema stage was lit. A group of young people were sitting on a dais at one side, near the grand piano where Mrs David was playing, her profile clear to Rachel. The piano's lid was closed so that the stage was visible to the *répétiteur*. Giuseppe Marcello was pacing to the music with a young woman hovering behind.

Rachel was intrigued in spite of herself and crept down the side aisle, then sat in about the tenth row, so that she could hear what was said; and now she saw that other people were listening from the first three rows, perhaps invited guests.

Nobody noticed her. Everybody was watching Marcello. Rachel could easily believe that he was a conductor, he grasped her attention so easily. Here he was using his whole body to demonstrate the music.

'You do not act this sadness,' he said. 'You feel it and your words are merely a means of expressing your loss. The husband you had thought faithful now looks elsewhere, flirts with your own maid, Susanna. It is not enough to sing the part.'

He turned to the students at the side of the stage: 'Today, perhaps more than ever, it is not enough to sing. The singer must be able to act also. Today, the cruel camera of television will show the singer who cannot make the character live, come to life for the listener watching in his own room, and rouse him from his own armchair. It is not enough to stand and give out the tune.' He arched his wrist back from his wide-open mouth. 'That will speak for itself. Mozart will even set the scene for you. We begin. Anna, please.'

Mrs David played the introduction, which was full of contrast, loud chords followed by soft, tremulous quavers.

'Note the tormented trills of her spirit. We will sing her, the Countess, in English, except when I forget! That will help our younger students, whose Italian commences. Now . . .' he called to the singer, a buxom young woman of about twenty. 'Suffer!'

She sang quite simply:

> God of love, I now implore thee
> Broken-hearted to thee I sigh,
> Love that once was mine restore me
> Or in mercy let me die.

On the word 'die', she paused on a high 'A'. Marcello stood beside her, willing her to hold the note, then cut off the last sound like a cobweb. Marcello shaped the repeated phrases with his hands, breathed with her, almost breathed into her part, it seemed to Rachel. As the Aria finished, the Countess sank her head in dejection.

'That is not bad at all. But just see this last phrase "O mi lascia almen morir", let it fade away to nothing. Let her willingly renounce her life if it is without love. Back to "love that once . . ."'

Mrs David started flawlessly, as if no directions were needed and she was thinking with Marcello. Again the Countess sang while Marcello pushed her shoulders into a drooping posture.

'Good. That will come. Now, after the impassioned prayer we jump to another sad Aria of the Countess, of nostalgia, when she looks back on the happiness she thinks may be lost for ever. With this, there is the problem of familiarity. This Aria is so well loved that it must be re-created, new, for your listener, as if you *were* the Countess, singing to herself, remembering for the sad pleasure. In the Recitativo, the Countess has told us how humiliated she feels herself, that she has been obliged to scheme with her servants, to trick this husband into admitting his faithless follies.'

Mrs David went on into the Aria, and Marcello half sang, half spoke the opening words: 'I remember days long departed, Days when love no end could know.' Then he broke off: 'Now darling, you. Remember!'

The Countess sang until she reached the allegro section. As the music quickened Marcello sprang beside her.

'Appassionato. "*Must* I languish all in vain?" You are not conquered. You hope to win him back. Yes. Come. Defiant. Throw up your head. And again. "*Faithless* heart regain." Now the exit. Not a march away, but regally, carried by your own fierce hope. You will fight. I like this Countess.'

'For the exit, Anna, please.'

They went through the movements several times, Marcello leading the Countess, holding both her hands, scowling her defiance at her until she laughed, and had to try again.

Although she was using the score, Rachel felt that her mother too was living the music, submerged in the opera, an essential part of its making, the bones beneath the skin.

'So much I want to try with you,' Marcello declared at last when he let the Countess go. 'Figaro's jealousy, all the magnificent intrigue of the garden in Act Four. But first, I have promised to hear one budding Cherubino.'

A tiny girl in a gathered skirt and frilled blouse came to the centre of the stage and sang. It was another Aria Rachel knew well: 'Tell me, fair Ladies, What stirs my heart?'

She had an astonishing voice. It was so dazzling, clear and really boylike. At the end of the Aria everyone applauded, and when Rachel saw her mother clapping and smiling she knew that she could not possibly interrupt this dedicated bliss. The quarrel with Cousin Luke would be an intrusion. It would be inconceivable to stop this Class to thrust their troubles before her, push their problems into her lap.

For it was 'their' problem, and up to them to put it right. Rachel sat and clenched her hands. Seeing her mother so absorbed and happy how could she interrupt so callously? This was her old London life, long rehearsals for the opera, the rest of the world cut off. If she could find some fresh happiness in returning to it, then they must stay in the London area, for her as well as for their schooling.

And Matthias and Tatiana were away, well away, tucked into another cinema. She would just have to tackle Cousin Luke on her own, before her mother came back. That was the least she could do. But it was more than she wanted to try. She was a little lonely, for she did not belong there, among the busy musicians. Rachel went out of the building, again unnoticed.

CHAPTER THIRTEEN

'I t's hard to know where I do belong,' Rachel reflected sadly, swinging the heavy door behind her and stepping into the front garden of Bridge House. But as she walked slowly to their side door, she realised that she herself wanted to belong to Bridge House. She had become attached to it, and could in some way understand Cousin Luke's devotion to the place, though not the extraordinary rages whose aftermath she felt obliged to tackle.

'I'll have a cup of coffee, then I'll go and try to make our peace with him,' she told herself. 'It's no good putting it off, because Matthias is angry and Tatiana frightened, so they wouldn't be much help. Except,' she added honestly, 'for moral support.'

When she went downstairs, she called first on Miss Drube and found that Cousin Luke was in.

'We had a bit of a row with him this morning,' Rachel said. 'Did you hear anything?'

'No; but I was out shopping, you see. And I had a look round the back this morning. You *have* made a difference. It's beginning to look like a garden again.'

Rachel smiled gratefully at Miss Drube. 'Thank you for saying so.'

'I'm not just saying it. I mean it,' Miss Drube assured her. 'By the by, I've been looking out something for you. If you'd like it, that is.'

'I'm sure I should,' Rachel said politely, not sorry in any

case to be delayed, as Miss Drube rummaged in her dresser drawer. 'Is it for all of us?'

'No, just for you, I should guess. That young Tatiana isn't one for getting her pretty hands dirty, and I don't expect she ever will, bless her.' Miss Drube smiled fondly to herself. 'That one'll always find plenty of young men later on, to run her errands.'

'I expect so,' said Rachel a little wistfully, wondering what homely object was going to be given to her as a suitable present. A coal glove? It would be nice to be brilliant and difficult sometimes, bursting out with musical talent or balletic brilliance, instead of what she felt today, a weary go-between.

'There it is. It's very old. But I had a notion you would like it.' Miss Drube pushed a handknitted puce tea cosy back into the drawer, and put a small book on the table in front of Rachel. It was a dull green, faded almost to khaki at the edges, but on the front a gold engraved circlet of flowers tied with fluttering ribbon enclosed the title:

EVERY LADY
Her Own
Flower
Gardener

Rachel was delighted and flattered. 'I'd love to look at it.'

'No. It's *for* you. You keep it if you fancy it. It's no use to me, in the drawer. I don't think I've opened it in years. I didn't buy it, you know. Mr David threw it out years ago, and I didn't like to see it go in the dustbin, so I put it away in the drawer.'

Rachel hardly heard what was being said. She opened the book, and smiled at the title page, severely 'addressed to the industrious and economical only', then turned a page, and was ravished.

It was as if she stepped into summer. From both sides of the page brilliant flowers glowed, their colours so bright and fresh that the petals looked wet, moistened with early dew. They were drawn with such loving exactitude, every leaf and stamen etched with care. She half expected to breathe in sweet scent from red, yellow, blue, orange, black, white and changing greens.

Rachel was transfigured. She could see why people spoke of the language of flowers, when these little paintings could so lift her spirits.

'Perhaps one day I could make the garden at Bridge House bloom,' she thought. 'Perhaps even next summer, I could sow something "economical", as well as herbs. I might have great pink peonies and gaudy anemonies. There could be clumps of fragrant lavender, climbing sweet peas, trailing honeysuckle, one day roses to cut and trim, blossoming trees and flowering shrubs. If only we stay. . . .'

'You like it then?' Miss Drube was looking at her anxiously.

'I love it,' Rachel said simply. 'I was just carried away, daydreaming of what this garden *could* be. Just dreaming.'

'Well, I'm glad you like it. And you carry on what you're doing. There's no reason why you shouldn't start a bit of life out of doors, is there?'

'There's plenty of life indoors, when the others get going,' Rachel now felt capable of saying, glancing through the book.

'It doesn't do any harm. The house needs livening up, as I've said to your Tatiana more than once.'

'"Snails are disagreeable intruders,"' Rachel read out. 'The author suggests that you throw cabbage leaves on to borders at night, and come and find the snails all over the underneath the next morning. Then slay them!' She pulled a face. 'Maybe I'll get some modern powder from a shop. I don't know that I'm brave enough to face snails or slugs in bulk!'

'I expect it's all very old-fashioned, donkey's years old.'

'Yes.' Rachel leafed to the front. 'It was written in 1840. But I do like it. And thank you for giving it to me. I'd better go and face Cousin Luke now. Try and speak to him, and get it over.'

Rachel felt unexpectedly encouraged and restored by the surprise present as she left Miss Drube. She braced herself once more. She had never been able to let quarrels last, had always been the first to 'make up' their earlier squabbles, but this was much harder. She found herself tapping rather feebly on Cousin Luke's door.

When he answered, she went in and found, as on their first meeting, that he was playing solitaire. He looked up at her and did not speak.

'Cousin Luke. I . . . We . . . I've come to apologise for this morning. We are sorry we disturbed you, as we know you don't like a lot of noise. You see, we thought you were out and. . . .'

'Your young sister was prancing on my stairs, against all my wishes, indeed my clear command.'

'I'm afraid she got excited and danced away downstairs without thinking.'

'She has, I fear, done herself great harm,' Cousin Luke said slowly.

'How do you mean? You won't forgive her for trespassing, disobeying you? I know she's sorry.'

'That will not save her.'

Rachel felt stupid and confused. They did not seem to be discussing the same thing. 'I don't think I understand you.'

'There is more in this house than bricks and stone, wood and glass. Old misfortunes come again.'

'You mean a sort of bad luck. I don't believe in bad luck,' Rachel said, bravely looking into his cold grey eyes.

'I did not, at one time, but the history of this house has induced me to change my mind. However, it is nearly at an end.'

Rachel thought of the great album she had seen. 'You are working on it, writing a history?'

'I am completing the history. I am the end of the history as well.'

'But history can't end,' Rachel protested.

'Sometimes it is better so,' Cousin Luke said stubbornly.

'Cousin Luke, I didn't come to argue,' she started again helplessly. 'What I came to ask is if you could give us another chance? Please, don't complain about us to our mother, although we did make a noise. And we will do our *very* best not to disturb you again.'

Cousin Luke waited for what seemed minutes.

'Very well. I shall say nothing. But in future please keep your sister away from that looking-glass. Perhaps it will be all right. We shall have to wait and see.'

'Thank you. I should like to help you in some way while we are here, if you would let me.' Rachel went pink as he looked up, clearly surprised.

'But you have already tended the garden, and I have observed that the London Pride is beginning to flower.'

And for the first time that she could remember, Cousin Luke smiled. Rachel was so amazed that she could hardly smile back. She gulped 'Thank you' again and hurried away startled, ran down the garden and gazed at the full river until she felt calm enough to return to the prosaic job of making tea.

*　　*　　*

Early that evening, Mrs David returned with Giuseppe Marcello.

'I've brought him for supper,' she told them. 'And we've shopped for food on the way home.'

'Another gateau?' Tatiana asked hopefully.

Marcello was laden with packets and now stood helplessly, not knowing what to do. So Rachel took them from him. He smiled at her and said:

'I'm sure you would divide it fairly. I wouldn't dream of trying,' he added. 'Two ice cream blocks into five would be much too difficult.'

Rachel was unpacking the packets. She looked surreptitiously at Marcello's handsome hair, which was shining dark, thick and rather long. It suited him, she decided, and the white was hardly visible. He seemed so vital that they were all vibrating with excitement at the unexpected party after such an unfortunate start to the day.

'How did the class go?' she asked him shyly.

'Your mother was brilliant, absolutely. Always she fol-

lowed. Sometimes she seemed to know before I did where we should start again. Never did she need to be told.'

'Oh, we have to tell her a thing or two sometimes, just to keep her in her place, you know,' Matthias said.

Rachel beckoned Matthias out of the kitchen where they were all milling round the laughing Mrs David.

'Wouldn't this be the moment? Why don't we give her the street piano now? It's working well enough, isn't it?'

'Of course. You clever girl!' Matthias produced more

admiration for this idea than for all her laborious reconciliation with Cousin Luke on their behalf. 'We'll take them in after supper.'

So after a hilarious meal, in which Marcello told a series of impossible stories about his travels over Yorkshire moors in thick fog to conduct lost orchestras, they went into the drawing-room to have coffee.

Tatiana, forewarned, opened the door with a flourish, and Matthias and Rachel trundled the street piano into the room loudly playing.

Mrs David sat back and laughed helplessly until they were almost afraid she would cry. Marcello sprang up and walked round the instrument, bouncing on his feet in delighted rhythm. Tatiana fluttered behind her mother:

'You do like it? You are surprised?'

'I'm staggered. What a gorgeous noise. And where did you get it? And how on earth up here?'

'When you were gadding at the opera . . .' Matthias gave a mock bow to Marcello, 'Rachel and I man-handled it. A crane through the window.'

'You didn't!'

'Up the stairs.'

'But which stairs? And Cousin Luke . . .' Mrs David protested a little anxiously.

'Oh that was all right. It's here now,' Rachel said quickly. 'And who do you think it's come from?'

'Not Jane and Viv?'

'Right first time! This accompanying lark has sharpened your old wits,' Matthias joked.

'But it is magnificent,' Marcello interrupted. 'Play some more, Matthias. After all, I shall not have it in my home. Unless you let me steal it away!'

'It's a birthday present for Mummy,' Tatiana reproached him.

'Then you will have to invite me again. Perhaps I could make a recording, Anna. It is a superb tone, so full. I should play it in the bath, and sing, when no one would hear.'

Matthias turned the handle and played for Marcello, who suddenly turned on Tatiana and whirled her into an exaggerated waltz, so that her hair, tied at the top of her head, spun out like a golden mane.

As the tune finished, Matthias offered: 'If you have a tape recorder, I could perhaps do a tape for you.'

'That would be magnificent. You must allow me to give you the tape. They are very costly. And then,' he wrinkled his eyes in a smile, 'I can ask for all the tunes! I have always longed to have a really *loud* mechanical instrument. For years I have looked for one of those early gramophones for outdoor use. You know them? Huge trumpet.' He circled with his hands.

'Yes, and sixteen-inch discs. I know the sort of thing. Come and see my lot. I'm afraid there's nothing as rare as that.'

Matthias took Marcello upstairs to show him all his precious equipment. Tatiana went to listen, and Rachel and her mother sat quietly together, having second cups of coffee.

'You did keep the secret well. A lovely present to end a lovely day.'

'A very gay ending. He's tremendous fun to have as a visitor,' Rachel said, glad that her mother had not come back to a complaint from Cousin Luke. He might even have asked them to leave. They were still within the agreed trial period. She sighed with private relief.

'Tired and happy? So am I. Really Giuseppe has that quality that while you are working with him nothing else matters, or hardly exists. You don't realise what's hit you till afterwards.'

'It was a good Class?'

'Wonderful. He's quite enthralled with a young student who's been studying Cherubino's part. He thinks she shows great promise, wants her to visit Italy, and for him she really did sing like an angel!'

'So you've been up the golden stairs to glory, accompanying her,' Rachel said teasingly.

'What made you say that? We always said it when you were little, and "Up the wooden hill to bed".'

'I must have stairs on the brain, living over Cousin Luke. I can imagine Marcello getting people to perform well. I wonder how he does it?'

'I think it's a combination of musicianship — he knows his *Figaro* backwards — and magnetism. He inspires people to do better than they thought they could. Mind you, I myself would need rest cures in between bouts of working with him. But it was lovely to be back for a while, then come home to you three. I wasn't sure how it would be, better or worse. But I felt nearer to your father again there.'

Rachel was determined not to let one note of sadness spoil her mother's day.

'Then Many Happy Returns to the Opera,' she said, and wondered if she would dream that night of Cousin Luke's unfamiliar, strained smile or the easy laughter of Giuseppe Marcello.

*   *   *

The next morning it was fine and Rachel went straight to the garden after breakfast to continue preparing a bed for herbs. If all went well, she hoped to plant them in April and May. And if they had to leave Bridge House then she would leave some roots behind, that was all. But very soon, she was driven indoors by a heavy shower. The others were still sitting over breakfast.

Matthias was telling Mrs David:

'And he's going to ask his friend if I can go and see his studio. Apparently, they've got masses of radiophonic equipment. The place is stuffed with it. I hope he doesn't forget.'

'Giuseppe won't forget. He is very kind to younger musicians. Not that he's so old himself! I'm sure he won't forget.'

'I'm glad you brought him back. I think I might make a recording for him this morning. I've got a spare tape.'

'I'm sure he'd be pleased. And you like him too, Tatiana? He knows quite a bit about ballet, doesn't he?'

'A lot,' Tatiana admitted, which was high praise. 'I thought he was charming.'

Matthias laughed at her. 'He would be flattered.'

Rachel said nothing. She had not dreamt of Cousin Luke. She wondered if Giuseppe Marcello was married to a beautiful Italian wife.

CHAPTER FOURTEEN

S o m e days later, there was a loud knock at the main front door followed by the bell ringing. This call was sufficiently unusual to rouse the Davids' curiosity, and Rachel, who had finished her breakfast, was sent out on the landing to see who it was.

To her surprise, Miss Drube opened the door to a policeman, and asked him into the hall after a short conversation. He was a large, awkward young man, who stood holding his helmet over the buckle at his waist, after saying a loud 'Thank you' to Miss Drube, who scuttled away towards Cousin Luke's room.

There was a pause, and then Cousin Luke came across the hall with deliberation, tapping away with his stick unhurriedly. Rachel leaned against the wall and unashamedly eavesdropped.

'Mr Luke David?'

'Yes.'

'Good morning, sir. The Port of London Authority has put out a warning of high tides, sir. And the police have been asked to warn all owners of riverside properties, particularly with basements, cellars, or low-lying rooms in use.'

'Bridge House has never been flooded in my lifetime,' Cousin Luke stated forbiddingly.

He turned away, but the young policeman repeated:

'We have been informed that the tide will be extra high,

sir, in about five hours or less. And people might get took by surprise. It will only be in these upper reaches of the river because there's a lot of water in the Thames Valley, a surge in the North Sea, and now this strong wind.'

Cousin Luke seemed neither impressed nor convinced. He managed to tower over the tall policeman.

'Never in my life time,' he repeated obstinately. 'Thank you, young man.'

The policeman knew himself to be dismissed, and decided that he had done his duty. 'Right you are, sir.' He clicked his thick shoes together and left the hall, shutting the front door behind him.

Rachel waited until Cousin Luke was back in his room before she moved from the wall, to which she almost felt glued.

'Well, who was it? The bailiffs, to throw us all out?' Matthias demanded.

'No, the police,' Rachel answered, enjoying their surprise.

'Why? What has he done?' Tatiana looked gleeful.

'Nothing, silly. It was just a constable, who had come to warn Cousin Luke that there'd be a very high tide today.'

'It wouldn't come up the garden, surely though,' Mrs David commented.

'Cousin Luke said that at once — that the House had never been flooded in . . .'

'I can imagine. He told the Thames to stay in its place,' Matthias interrupted, laughing.

'But Bridge House hasn't basements in use, or cellars,' Rachel went on. 'Still, the policeman stuck to his guns and gave the message, as they're warning all owners of riverside property.'

'Quite a job. I suppose the river police launches are out too.'

'It's a nasty thought for those little houses on the towpath,' Mrs David said. 'I wouldn't welcome that dirty water into any living-room of mine.'

'Filthy,' Tatiana shuddered. 'We'll be all right, won't we?'

'Ninny! A high Spring tide isn't going to come over the banks, up the garden and into the first floor,' her brother said scornfully.

'But there's Miss Drube's rooms. You go down three steps to the kitchen.'

'Oh, they'll be all right. It's got to come up the garden first,' Mrs David pointed out. 'But we'll tell her, just to set your mind at rest.'

'I think we should,' Rachel agreed. 'There's no harm done, though I'll have to admit eavesdropping.'

'Don't worry. Probably her ears were on stalks from the back of the hall,' Matthias said. 'She knew she'd get no news out of the old man.'

'Poor old man. It's his home,' Rachel reflected, accidentally thinking aloud.

'And don't we know it,' Matthias added.

'Never mind. It's a big help to us, tides or no tides. Now, what are you all doing this morning? Tatiana, class, isn't it? And you'll be back for a late lunch.'

'Yes.'

'I'll see to that,' Rachel offered, 'because I'm going to garden all morning, if this wind holds the rain off.'

'Could it be cold lunch?' Matthias asked. 'Because I'm going later on to a second-hand shop, and I don't know when I'll be back, but I can't afford to eat out.'

'Take sandwiches if you like,' his mother suggested. 'I shan't be late, Rachel, but you know what Giuseppe is. I'll have an early snack, then go off to the recording studio and hope to be back for tea.'

'This is for the Cherubino girl, isn't it?'

'Yes. He wants to take some recordings home with him — cheaper than her fare after all — to play to the Manager of his Opera House, then perhaps send for her at the end of her term, in the summer.'

'How exciting, to go to Italy,' Tatiana said wistfully.

'I expect you'll dance all over the world. You've chosen a good career for travelling, if that's what you want,' Mrs David said. 'And Lisa is only a student.'

'She's awfully good though, isn't she? I thought so when she practised with you,' Rachel said.

'Quite exceptional. We're doing some very difficult modern things too. She just throws out that voice. I don't know where it all comes from!'

'I got a bit of her on tape, but I only had the end of one left, and didn't want to rub out the rest. Do you think he'd let me in to listen?' Matthias asked. 'If I came on there?'

'I'm sure he would. It's at the Arbutus Studios, Hanover Street. Booked for one-thirty onwards.'

'I know them. I've been there before, with Daddy.'

Rachel noticed that Matthias mentioned their father without difficulty. The success of his visit to the sound studio arranged by Giuseppe seemed to have settled him firmly into what he wanted to do. And he was now ready to go out and try to do things with his sort of music. She hoped she'd be able to appear enthusiastic, or be at least convincingly polite about the results, when they came.

'Good. Then we're all settled,' Mrs David said. 'The holidays are going fast. Shall I make you some sandwiches then, Matthias?'

'Yes, please.'

'Could I have a couple for elevenses?' Tatiana asked. 'I'll go and tell Miss Drube about the high tide while you make them. Then I must go, or I'll be late for class.'

'Which would be the end of the world!' Matthias called

after her. 'It's fantastic how keen these girls are. Flogging away at the same old routine, voluntarily, in their holidays, bending and stretching, contorting themselves in front of mirrors and so on.'

'It's like everything else. They love every minute of it, but it seems crazy to the uninitiated,' Mrs David remarked.

'Except for the results,' Rachel added. 'When you see real dancers, you can understand anyone with talent working hard to achieve anything as beautiful as ballet.'

'And some dancers make their own ballets, which must be even better,' her mother agreed. 'You don't have to retire from choreography.'

'Nor gardening,' Rachel said with some satisfaction, and went off down the back stairs, well wrapped up in a sweater, old jeans and a cast-off mac which had belonged to Matthias.

She went straight down to the river. It was extremely full. She had never seen the water level with the path, and now it was only a few inches below the stones at the top of the bank, carrying twigs and driftwood in its fast, grey-brown swirling stream. But the length of their garden stood between the river and the house, even if it crept beneath the gate, or seeped through cracks in the wall. She was glad of the wall, for the river mud would probably sweep away her small efforts at gardening.

As she walked up the garden again, she heard the front door slam. From the side of the house she saw Cousin Luke walk down the front path, without a backward glance. He was not going to look at the river. It was his morning for going out, and only a cloudburst or a thunderbolt, she decided, would stop him.

The other three went out, and Rachel worked contentedly through the morning, rescuing a clump of lilies of the valley from a massive straggle of weeds by the wall, smelling the wet earth and feeling the wind on her face and neck.

Some time later, she heard footsteps on the front path, and went round to see who was calling.

It was the same policeman, and he smiled at her, with a relieved look.

'I wonder if I could leave a message with you? Save me troubling the old gentleman again.'

'Certainly.' Rachel smiled at him sympathetically.

'Well, you see, we've been sent to give a second warning. The tide's coming in faster than expected. We've heard of a river wall cracking down at Horseferry Wharf in Rother-hithe. The Fire Brigade's alerted. Our vans are out with loudspeakers, too. It's taken people by surprise, because usually the tide rises at Southend. Gives people time to be prepared. And it's inches higher than expected today. Already.' His voice rose a little.

Rachel realised that inches would count if the water could run down or fill up holes and crevices. She had vague memories of beach damming, and complicated defences against the incoming tides, with Matthias issuing frantic orders for her to 'Block up that leak' in their walls of sand.

'I'll let Mr David know when he comes back,' she told the policeman. 'He's out at the moment, up in London.'

The young man relaxed visibly. 'Well, you should be all right here, I suppose. But I should take a look round the downstairs rooms for valuables which could be damaged, if I were you.'

'They are his, and his housekeeper's,' Rachel explained. 'But I'll tell her. Just in case.'

'You two are in on your own?' The young man hesitated. 'I've got to go right along this stretch again, but I'll try to call back and give you a hand, in case you need help. Though

I may get caught up. You can always give the Station a ring.'

'We haven't a 'phone, but don't worry. We'll be all right. Mr David is an old man, and it's never reached the house in his lifetime.'

'I expect there'll be plenty of voluntary helpers if we do have trouble,' said the policeman, with some relish. 'I must be off. And you'll tell him I called?'

'I will,' Rachel promised, and returned to her gardening.

But his subdued excitement had made her restless, and she went down again to the river. Now the water was lapping over the path, and she stood staring at it, watching how quickly it encroached on new land.

*　　*　　*

An hour and a half later the alley at the side of Bridge House was a stream, and water was running into the back garden. A crack in the side wall was admitting a steady trickle which was waterlogging the grass.

Rachel stood in wellington boots, fascinated and horrified. She had walked out into Aynescombe Green to find out what she could. People were standing in the street watching drains overflowing. She went into the newspaper shop, and heard them gossiping about the swollen river reaching nearly to the top of the parapets on the terrace of the Houses of Parliament.

'And that *is* high,' said the shopkeeper, with gloomy satisfaction. 'There'll be a lot of people in a mess by to-night. The tide's not finished yet. Not by a long way. I'm glad I'm this side of the road. I never did fancy the river side. You never know. Might get them rats.'

Rachel decided against buying anything, and drifted along the road to a small turning down to the river, leading

to a pub and some houses. As she had expected, the river
had swept into the dip of the road. But she had not expected to find parked cars with their wheels covered by
water. Children were paddling gleefully in the new lake;
little girls had tucked up their dresses to wade in as far as
possible. Small boys were riding at the edges of the water,

as deep as they dared, putting their feet up on the cross-
bar as they freewheeled splashingly.

Everywhere there was an uneasy excitement, as if it was
all right so long as the river didn't come too far, get out of
hand and spoil the best carpet. Rachel returned to the part
she knew best, by Bridge House, where she could most
easily judge the water's advance.

It was relentless. The front garden was now in shallow

muddy water. The back garden had pools and a running stream. Rachel walked round the house, and came to the french windows of Cousin Luke's secret room, shuttered as usual. But would, she wondered, the old windows hold out this insidious rising water? Would it creep between the cracks, and cover Amelia's pink boudoir with greeny slime?

There was only one way to make sure. Rachel ran indoors.

CHAPTER FIFTEEN

S H E did not stop to consult Miss Drube, but ran straight-way to the secret room. It was locked. Feeling unreasonably upset, she ran back to the kitchen. The water wasn't very deep, she told herself, but somehow she wanted to protect the heart of the house for the old man. Even if almost embalmed, frozen so many years ago, it was precious to him. As she had found out his retreat by chance, she now felt protective towards it.

Miss Drube was not in the kitchen. Rachel called out: 'Miss Drube, are you there?'

She hurried into her personal room, dashed up the back stairs to their part of the house, calling and panting, but nobody was in.

Perhaps Miss Drube was shopping, or had felt impelled to see the strange sights, as Rachel had, and had relied on Cousin Luke being away until his usual time of return.

'By then,' Rachel worked out, 'the tide may have turned, but what will it have left behind? I wish I knew when high tide was due. But I suppose it would all be different today anyhow. What damage the river can do in a short time. Though it's never reached the house in his lifetime, it has done today, with a vengeance. It'll pass the eighteenth-century high-water mark the way it's going. History repeating itself.'

She plodded downstairs in her wellingtons, and stopped

in the hall. Water had trickled under the old doors and a thin layer of mud touched the foot of the stairs. Rachel remembered Cousin Luke's album, resting open on a low table. Could the water reach that? Surely not. But she could not tell how much the shutters would let in. And there were steps down into the room.

She rushed up to Cousin Luke's door and heaved against it with all her weight, longing for Matthias's strength to force the door, or his handiness to pick the lock. She prowled out into the garden, where the water seemed deeper, and peered anxiously round the shutters, wondering if it were worth trying to 'sand-bag' the outside, block up all the crannies with earth or mud, or whatever she could find.

'I'd rather get in the room,' Rachel decided. 'I wish that policeman'd come back. Or a fireman. They force doors if you need it. I remember Tatiana locking herself in the lavatory at a party, and the fireman came and sawed through the bolt while Mummy talked to her through the little window. And she just ran out and hugged the fireman and danced round in his helmet while poor Daddy gave our "Particulars" to the chief officer.'

Rachel wondered if she could possibly trouble the police or Fire Brigade to protect a room and its treasures, when they might be saving people's lives. She went into the kitchen, looked vainly for keys or a file, or any tool to bash at the door, but there was nothing she felt she could manage; and she really hadn't the nerve to start smashing out windows to force the shutters open. Rachel paddled out into the road, and noticed how quiet it was. The lower end near the Green might be blocked by water or a diversion, she guessed, for she could hear footsteps and talking instead of heavy traffic, while water ran silently down the kerbs. Rachel watched helplessly.

Then she had a piece of luck. 'Her' policeman came cycling slowly along. Rachel called out:

'Please, I say.'

He stopped his bike. 'Hello. In trouble?' He looked thrilled, ready for anything.

Rachel was delighted to see him. 'Oh please, could you give me some help? I can't get into one of our rooms. It's locked, and there are valuables inside. Could you break open the door for me?'

'Well, we do reckon to tackle anything, but . . . we police don't usually break and enter, you know! Let's have a look-see.'

They went into the hall, now inches deep in water.

'It's in here all right,' the policeman said appreciatively, as if he rather admired the river's audacity, invading the formidable Mr David's property, in his absence. 'It's not like releasing someone trapped, now is it though?' he said when they reached the door and Rachel explained the position.

'But there are valuable things there. Very old. And a book. Only *one* copy of it. I'll take the blame,' she added.

'Not with my chief you won't. But here goes.'

He took out a small metal tool, knelt down by the door and fiddled energetically. In fact, the lock was an old one and collapsed easily. Rachel pushed open the door, and gasped with relief. The history album was unharmed. There were four or five inches of water, but the low table was clear. Rachel snatched up the book. 'Oh, thank you. I can manage now.'

He was staring round. 'Old-fashioned, isn't it. Falling to pieces a bit. Does anyone *use* it?'

'Yes, in a way. It's been kept like this a long time, I think.'

'The carpet'll need a bit of a clean-up. Pink was it once?'

He looked down at the sodden, grey, muddy floor-covering. 'A funny little room. More like a museum than a parlour really or a little lounge. Now I'd better leave you my name and number in case there's any bother.' He scribbled on a piece of paper torn from his pad. 'I must be off,' he said, but stared round the little room again before he left.

'Goodbye, and thank you very much indeed. You may not get the chance again to break into a house by invitation!' Rachel said.

'Oh, we get all sorts in this job,' he told her cheerfully.

As soon as he left, Rachel applied herself to clearing the room, lifting up everything that looked at all valuable on to the top of a narrow tallboy. She took the Album upstairs, then the music box and Amelia's portrait. Now she was inside the room she was no longer worried, because she could be ahead of the river. She was so occupied that she did not hear Miss Drube coming, and turned, startled, when she spoke:

'Rachel, how did you get in there? What *will* Mr David say? Just look at the mess!'

'I have been,' Rachel answered mildly. 'I think even he'll realise it's not our fault.'

'But he won't have anyone in this room. I'm only allowed in once a *month* to clean it through. And then he stands over me half the time as if I'm going to steal the knicknacks.'

'They mean so much to him, I suppose. All he's got left. That's why I wanted to make sure they weren't ruined by river water, as I knew they were here.'

'But how? It's always kept locked. I think he comes here mostly in the evenings, or at night, if he can't sleep.'

'I know.'

Rachel explained as quickly as she could, emptying the room as she talked. Miss Drube, too dumbfounded to give much help, clucked away to herself when she heard about Tatiana.

'Frightened her to death he did. And then about the mirror too. I was telling her this morning that she mustn't trouble her little head about these old tales. All worked up she was. But she wouldn't listen to me.'

Rachel only half listened too. She was planning how to leave the room, wondering if she ought to stay in the hall and meet Cousin Luke, to warn him. She wished that her mother or at least one of the others would come in first, but, once again, she would have to face him. Only this time, surely, he couldn't be angry.

CHAPTER SIXTEEN

Rachel was at the back of the hall when Cousin Luke came home. She heard the front door being opened, and shut. Then there was complete silence. She waited. Still there was silence. She walked towards the front door and found Cousin Luke leaning against it, looking white and frail, the old man he really was.

'My house, Rachel,' was all he managed to say.

'It is a shock at first, but honestly, everything's safe.' She went up to him and guided him over to the hall chair, where he sat down without resisting her help in any way. He seemed shrivelled, and gazed bleakly at the muddy floor.

'The damage. It could never be repaired.' He tried to get up, but appeared too overcome to leave the chair and go and see for himself.

'It was just an exceptionally high tide,' Rachel said gently. 'But soon it will turn, then the water will subside. The Fire Brigade said that they couldn't do much till then, when they'd see where the pockets of water had collected, and pump it out.' He winced, and she went on quickly: 'We're all right here. The cellars aren't in use.'

'But I have a room unknown to you, leading from this hall. It was once a little conservatory. And lies lower than the other rooms. It will be swamped, saturated.'

He would have to know some time, and for the moment he was not unapproachable as he normally was. 'You mean the pink room,' she stated, trying to sound composed.

'Amelia's room. How do you know of it? How could you?' he asked in bewilderment.

'Everything's quite safe,' Rachel repeated. 'I did know about it because I came down here one night, to track down the music from the music box. Tatiana was scared it was ghosts,' she explained with embarrassment, 'and it was the only way to reassure her. The door was open. You were asleep and I saw your music box, the portrait, the Album, the whole room. I know it sounds dreadful, walking in like that, but it has done some good.' She looked at him appealingly.

'How?'

'When I saw that the river water *was* coming into the house I realised that it might leak through the shutters or somewhere else. I didn't know the room well enough to tell what might happen.'

'But it was locked. I have the key.'

'We broke in. And the Album is safe. And the music box. And the portrait.'

'Where?'

'Upstairs. It really did seem the best thing to do. The water's so filthy, and we couldn't stop it, or know when it would stop by itself. I . . .'

Cousin Luke had forced himself to stand, and walked squelchily over his hall, putting the stick on to the slippery surface with great care.

He opened the door of the pink room and stepped inside. Rachel stood behind him as he spoke to himself:

'Now the river has even driven her from here.'

Rachel hesitated.

'Cousin Luke. Miss Drube is in the kitchen, and we'll both clean up as soon as the tide turns. But wouldn't you like to come upstairs and rest now for a while?'

133

He turned and looked at her with a dazed expression.

'None of the others is in. Won't you come upstairs just for a little while?'

He nodded slowly, and they walked together up the wide stairs, past the black curtain and into the Davids' sitting-room, without saying a word. Rachel left him sitting upright in an armchair, with both hands holding his stick, staring blankly ahead.

She made tea hastily, came back and poured out a cup for him.

'Do you take sugar, Cousin Luke?'

He nodded. As he drank, Rachel sat down and waited, in case he wanted to speak.

'Where are they?'

'Who, the others? Well, Mummy's playing the piano for a recording, and Matthias may be joining her after looking for some radio equipment. Tatiana . . .'

'The inquisitive little girl.'

'She's at a dancing class this morning.'

'It is afternoon now,' Cousin Luke said precisely.

Rachel looked at the clock for the first time. It was a quarter-past two.

'Good heavens, where on earth has she got to? Dawdling around, gossiping to her teacher, I suppose. But she did say she'd be in for a late lunch. I expected her before half-past one. I hadn't realised. . . .'

'She is all right?' Cousin Luke asked sharply.

'Oh, yes.' Rachel fidgeted uncomfortably, as he had resumed his usual manner. 'Just a bit late. Perhaps traffic has been dislocated by flooding.'

'I hope so. My train ran normally,' Cousin Luke replied. 'Can your sister swim?'

Rachel was surprised, then concerned. 'Yes, a bit. Why do you ask? I'm sure she's not going to go swimming in the river today because it's flooded. Much too dirty for her. And too cold!'

'Does she know about the mirror on the stairs?' he asked insistently.

'Well, she saw it the day we were in trouble with you for making that noise.' Rachel began to wonder if the shock had turned his wits, but he seemed perfectly lucid.

'Have you seen the mirror?'

'Not properly.'

'Then go and look in it now, for yourself.'

Rachel felt compelled to do as he told her. She walked down to the head of the stairs, drew back the black curtain and saw a large, rectangular mirror, about nine feet high. The frame was carved gilt wood adorned with elaborate scrolls of ferny leaves. The top ornament was a golden swam, swimming within a circlet of decorative reeds. Along the bottom of the frame, a gold painted panel was covered with black engraved writing. She stooped to read the words.

> Look not in this looking-glass
> Which came by water to this place,
> For she who sees the youngest face
> Should fear the river's cold embrace.
>
> High Tide, Spring,
> 1767.

For no reason she could explain, Rachel felt chilled. She let the curtain drop back. It was only, she told herself, the dank flood water below, the smell of the river, that made her shiver as she went slowly back to Cousin Luke.

He had not moved.

'I've seen the mirror. It is a beautiful one; a pity to hide it,' she said steadily.

'It is what lies behind it that we cannot see.'

Rachel firmly poured herself a cup of tea, trying not to long for her mother to come back, immediately, and take over this strange old gentleman. She would gladly have mopped out the hall and all the downstairs rooms single-handed, or with Miss Drube, if she could disengage herself from him for a while.

'Rachel, if that foolish child is drowned, I shall be the cause. I shall hold myself responsible.'

'She won't be drowned,' Rachel stated curtly. 'And how could you cause such a thing?'

'I should have explained to you all that she was in danger. The inscription was for a purpose, a warning. That mirror has always been unlucky.'

'But that wouldn't hurt Tatiana. And "bad luck" is just superstition.' Rachel warmed her hands round the tea pot.

'I, too, believed that at one time. However, when that mirror was brought to the house, it was brought by river.

In the late eighteenth century roads were so poor, it was smoother and safer for expensive glass to be transported by water. As it says in the verse:

"Which came by water to this place . . ."

But on the day it was installed, the youngest daughter of the house died. . . .'

'But that was obviously a coincidence,' Rachel protested.

'So you would think. But in every generation, the youngest female of our family has died an unnatural or early death. One fell down these stairs and broke her neck, and . . .'

'People just add to those stories.'

'Hear me out. So I believed, and I was obstinate in that belief. When my young bride came to live in our family home, she wanted to be rid of the mirror. I refused, because it was a beautiful object.' His mouth twisted. 'She pleaded. I would not give in. Finally, she ran away because she was frightened of the "spell", as she called it, of the mirror.'

'But you were right. Mirrors don't have spells.'

'I was merely obstinate.'

'You mean, you didn't persuade her to come back.' Rachel thought of the lovingly preserved pink room. 'You never tried?'

'No. I would not ask her to come back. Then, one year later, in the Spring, she was coming back of her own free will to visit me. I hoped, I allowed myself to hope, for a reconciliation. She slipped from the river path and was drowned. By the unexpected perilous high Spring tides.'

Rachel was appalled. It seemed such a waste, such needless devastation. 'How horrible! But that wasn't because of the mirror. It was just coincidence.'

'How can we be sure? I would not believe in her fears and that was the result.'

'But she left you because you were so pigheaded,' Rachel

exclaimed, and then stopped. 'Oh, heavens, what have I said?'

'What you thought, I imagine!' And to her astonishment, he almost smiled. 'You know, I had rejected everyone after that. Having failed her, I wished for no one else to be close to me, to be at risk. I worked, and studied this place, its history, and all the stories surrounding it. I did my daily work and came back here. Gradually, my friends accepted that I preferred this isolation. And, having lost Amelia, I did. It was my wish to be alone with her memory, to solve for myself the problem of the history of this place. Yet I have not fully succeeded in that, although I rejected this age, watching it become noisier and more thoughtless week by week and year by year. I withdrew completely.'

'Until you had us here. Why did you ask us?' Rachel was emboldened to ask now he was talking so freely.

'Murdoch persuaded me. He took no notice of my protests, threatened that I would lose Miss Drube and have no one to keep on the place. I could neither endure to leave it, nor to see it completely neglected, and yet I could not find people to work here. The local people had become, as you say, "superstitious" about it. I could hardly, as he pointed out, clean the house myself. Murdoch suggested tenants. I refused. Then he told me about your family. I felt I could have you, as distant relations, in the house without selling out its rooms as if it were a lodging house.'

He looked disdainful, and Rachel thought ruefully of their poor little flat, which had been so expensive for them.

'In short, he persuaded me. And you know the rest. You came, with your mother. I cut you off from the staircase and the fateful mirror. I thought that would suffice.'

'I'm sure it's not fateful,' Rachel said, though even as she spoke she caught herself hoping that Tatiana did *not* know the stories about the mirror.

'I hope it is not. I assure you that I should like to be proved wrong. But where *is* your young sister?'

'I'll go down and see if there's any sign of her in a minute. We could do with a telephone,' Rachel said bluntly, then added, in a more conciliatory tone, 'You'll be all right here? The music box, the big Album, the portrait, they're all up here.'

'I did not think that anyone was as considerate as that, in these days. I cannot see why you troubled.'

'It was nothing. I knew that they were there, and valuable to you.'

'But it is the history of *my* house.'

'I like the house, too,' Rachel told him brusquely, her mind on Tatiana. 'And it was the least I could do to save them.'

'I had rejected this generation,' Cousin Luke said.

'Well, you'd given us a home, don't forget. In any case, you can't reject the times you're living in. As long as you're alive in them, you're part of them. And there *are* marvellous things going on in the world.'

'What?'

Rachel stood over him, carried away by her own enthusiasm. 'Great advances in medicine, for just one thing. Cures of terrible diseases which used to kill people off, children too. I'll lecture you one day when I've time!'

'They can't cure old age,' Cousin Luke said.

'No, but they can ease it. And so could we yours, if you would let us!'

She shot out of the room, and defiantly down the main stairs before he could answer. She was *not* going to be frightened by him or his stories, although she did make a point of holding on to the banister, so that *she* could not fall and break her neck.

Miss Drube was in the kitchen and had no news of Tatiana.

'She went off to her class as usual this morning, just after she'd been in here, telling me about the high tide. And I hear it's twenty-six inches higher than they expected. Terrible, isn't it.'

'And she was all right?'

'Yes, I think so. She did seem a bit nervous about it, but I told her it had never come in the house yet. Which shows me up! Look at the muck in here. And the smell!'

'Miss Drube, did Tatiana ask you any more about the mirror on the stairs? Did she know the old superstitions about it?'

'She did, Rachel, though I let her know that I, for one, thought them nothing more than a pack of old stories. She was always on at me for all the tales, even though they scared her more than a bit.'

'Silly kid to pester you, but I know what she's like. It's just that she's very late, and I was getting a bit anxious, you see. Of course, she could have stayed out deliberately to worry us.'

'Would you like me to go out and have a look round for her?' Miss Drube offered. 'I couldn't rest here now. She may just be watching at the river. There's a lot going on.'

'But she could easily have come in for lunch and gone out again. Cousin Luke's been talking so much about the mirror he's made me worried now.'

'Then I'll go. Don't you bother.'

But as she spoke there was a deafening knock at the front door. The bell was clanged, too.

Miss Drube gasped.

Rachel felt violently sick, and stood in mute dismay.

CHAPTER SEVENTEEN

MISS DRUBE was there first, and opened the door to an ambulance man, who was carrying Tatiana in his arms, wrapped in a dark grey blanket.

'All yours, Miss,' he said cheerfully. 'Had a bit of an unexpected swim, but she's none the worse for it. We took her to the first-aid post, to make sure. But she's right as rain now.'

'Thank you,' Rachel stammered.

'Can you take over now, Miss, because we're that busy.'

'Yes, of course,' Rachel pulled herself together.

'Where shall I take her? Got a sofa or something that's still dry?'

'We're in the upstairs flat. But we can . . .'

Rachel found herself talking to his back. He was striding in a marvellously matter of fact way up the special stairs, unconcernedly leaving black footprints on the carpet. She tottered behind him weakly, managing to direct him to Tatiana's bedroom.

'There,' he said, and put her down on the bed so that she was propped against the bedhead. 'Now you'll be all right. And I must get on. Get a string of calls all night, I expect. Goodbye, Blondie.'

Tatiana smiled at him. 'Thank you very much.'

Her dirty hair looked lank and was still wet, hanging over her pale face, streaked with mud.

'Not much of a blondie till you've had a bath.' Rachel

gazed at her with aching relief. She looked so wan that it
seemed brutal, but the question had to be asked: 'What on
earth happened to you? It's long past two.'

'Nothing really. It sounds so stupid. I was coming home
from class, and, on the way back from the station. I saw a
crowd looking down that lane leading to the river. So I
went down to have a look. They were watching the high
tide coming in so fast. But I thought I could just get along
the river path home, and come up our alley by the house
here. I was just crossing the end of the lane on that low
wall, and I skidded on some mud, where the tide had been,
and fell in. Not very deep water. Just stupid. In that slopey
bit. But there was a terrible fuss. And they insisted on seeing
nothing was broken, when all I wanted was to come home.
To Mummy. Or you.'

Rachel was touched. 'You're all right now.'

'I was then. Just filthy and wet. I told them, but they wouldn't believe me. They wanted a bit more excitement.'

'You did bang your head.' Rachel noticed a red mark on Tatiana's forehead.

'Just a graze. I'm fine, honestly.'

She was a little surprised that Tatiana was so determined to minimise her extraordinary return home. It was unlike her, but Rachel merely said:

'The best thing for you now is a bath. I'll run one for you, if you get into your dressing-gown.'

'That'd be lovely.'

Rachel hurried out of the room, thinking hard. She put the bath water on, and went into the living-room, where Cousin Luke still sat motionless.

'That was Tatiana. She's quite all right. Just a bit muddy. Fell down in a flooded lane.'

'Thank heaven she is safe. It was the river then,' Cousin Luke added to himself.

'She's quite all right,' Rachel repeated. 'I'll come back. She's just going to have a bath, to warm her up.'

While she helped Tatiana, Rachel pondered. Tatiana was immensely relieved. She recognised the same feelings as her own. As soon as Tatiana was comfortably changed into dry clean clothes, she decided to straighten it out.

'Tatiana, why did you go down to the river?'

'To see the floods. On the train home, I'd seen the banks overflowing. There was a sort of weir on to a playing-field, so it looked like two rivers, spreading out like a lake, or a mere. And there was water up to car windows round one of the piers, with swans swimming round them, and . . .' She tailed away, as Rachel was looking at her reflectively. 'What is it?'

'But the flood wasn't the only reason. Tatiana; Cousin Luke is sitting next door in the living-room.'

'Why?' Tatiana looked uneasy.

'His part of the house is in a mess, needless to say, and I brought him, and some of his valuables up here, away from the water, till we can clear up. He's been very anxious about you, too.'

'I don't know why. He hates me.'

'He doesn't,' Rachel replied patiently. 'He's been frightened for you. That's all, really.'

'He should leave me alone. And I'll leave him, and his mirror alone.'

Rachel pursued her questioning. 'Why his mirror?'

'Because he makes such a fuss about it.'

'Come on. Tell. You know,' Rachel said firmly, 'we can't go on living here like this, with scenes on his stairs every five minutes, can we? And I, for one, want to stay here.'

'I suppose it will be all right for me now I've proved it,' Tatiana admitted reluctantly. 'And I do want to stay here, at least until I've taken the scholarship. Even then, I think they might want me to live at home, as we're in the London area.'

'But what were you trying to prove to yourself?' Rachel was unyielding.

'That I *would* be safe in the high tide even though I had looked in the mirror and read the verse.'

'You didn't believe those old stories?'

'Not exactly, but I thought that the only way to be sure was to try. So I sort of dared myself to walk along the river bank from Ship Lane to our house, to break the spell.'

'Brave in a silly way. Why didn't you say anything?'

'I was waiting for a high tide. And plucking up courage. And anyhow, you'd have stopped me. And Cousin Luke must have believed the stories too. So I wasn't *so* silly,' she finished defiantly.

'Yes, he did. At least, he feared they were true, that something could come to harm you if you looked in that mirror. It couldn't, but the whole thing's not quite so ridiculous when he tells it, because he's been studying the house over all these years, and there have been some odd coincidences. So by now I'm sure the past is as clear to him as the present. He's made, you see, the stairs a sort of barrier between our family and him. It's become a sort of habit. Not that that's an excuse for you, or me.'

Suddenly, Rachel realised what she must do. Talking to Tatiana had clarified the present situation for her. And that was what mattered most.

'We can clear this up with Cousin Luke now, and I think we should. Now, before the others get back.'

Tatiana looked alarmed. 'I couldn't. I feel tired now. I think I ought to have a rest.'

'You're fine. You said so yourself,' Rachel said unsympathetically. 'Come and see him, get it over. Honestly, he won't bite. The flood has tamed the tiger.'

Tatiana would not smile, but she followed her sister reluctantly into the next room. She stood in the doorway with her feet turned out.

Cousin Luke studied her, and then said simply: 'I am glad that you are safe, child.'

'Thank you.'

He turned to Rachel. 'You see the resemblance?'

She shook her head, confused.

'Look at the portrait of Amelia.'

Rachel looked from the picture to Tatiana. There was a certain likeness, she remembered, and now it came sharply into focus. This far-removed cousin, a young woman in an old-fashioned dress, could have been Tatiana's older sister. For their colouring was the same, and the setting of their deep blue eyes identical. Both girls stared at Rachel and Cousin Luke.

'This is a portrait of my wife,' he explained to Tatiana, in a quiet remote voice. 'My wife, Amelia. She was drowned in the river, in such a tide as this.'

'But only by chance, by accident, I am sure,' Rachel put in emphatically. If Cousin Luke could be obstinate, so could she. Now they had Tatiana restored safely, she could be even more definite to herself and to them. She went on doggedly: 'I think it would be pure superstition to blame the mirror, which is only a sheet of looking-glass in a frame of golden wood, for any misfortune in the past or the present.'

Tatiana was not so assured. 'Do you think the unlucky spell is broken now?' she asked Cousin Luke directly.

'I think that it must be,' he answered with a strange note in his voice.

Rachel was not sorry to hear footsteps on the stairs: she welcomed an interruption of such a difficult conversation.

Her mother and Matthias came in, with their own flood stories. On such an extraordinary day, while boats floated down the streets of Aynescombe Green, it did not seem so odd that Cousin Luke should stay to tea.

*   *   *

During that evening, a telegram arrived for Rachel. She could not believe that the day could hold any more shocks, but was very pleased to read:

PLEASE RING ME AT OPERA AS SOON AS POSSIBLE GIUSEPPE.

She explained to the others, and hurried out, down the muddy road to the nearest 'phone box. As soon as she spoke, Giuseppe said:

'Rachel. You are all right?'

'Yes, of course. Yes, I mean, thank you.'

'The beautiful house was not flooded? I had read such terrifying reports in the evening paper, and could not come out to help you. And, with no telephone, I felt. . . .'

His voice faded away uncharacteristically. It sounded much more foreign on the 'phone, Rachel thought, although she still liked it.

'Some water came in downstairs, and there is still some clearing up to do. But no great damage. And we're all safe. I was in when the water was rising. That was a bit alarming, and you couldn't stop watching it.'

'You were in alone?' he asked quickly.

'Only at first. Then the rest of the family came back. Tatiana, rather unconventionally, in the arms of an ambulanceman!'

Rachel told him the story. It was a relief to pour it out, and somehow, she was able to do so, on the 'phone, when she might have been shy and tongue-tied, looking at Marcello. And he did not seem bored by the long account, questioned her on every detail. Finally, she said:

'It was nice of you to telegraph me. Perhaps one day we'll persuade Cousin Luke to have a 'phone in the house.'

'I hope so. To be in touch with you all, and Anna's accompanying when I visit London, now I have discovered her. I decided to speak to you, Rachel, rather than your mother, because I thought that she might be too proud to ask if help were needed. I relied on you to tell me exactly, to admit any difficulty.'

He was after her good sense, like everyone else, Rachel thought, and shrugged. What else did she expect?

'Unless you count coping with Tatiana and the old man, as Matthias calls him, a difficulty? But I think that's going to be all right now. Perhaps.'

'I am assured that it will be, when you have finished with them,' Giuseppe said. 'I am confident in you.'

Rachel suddenly felt as if she were laughing inside. She saw her face in the mirror of the 'phone box. Her cheeks were unusually pink, and her eyes bright, as if she had emerged from darkness to light.

'And Matthias,' she said incoherently. 'He's going to be all right too. Since you took him to hear that radiophonic music, he's been a different person. He says he knows what he's going to do, and working with that would be his idea of heaven. Incredible to me,' she admitted, then wished she had left it unsaid.

But Giuseppe laughed, and she wished that she could see him, just for a minute.

'Rachel, you stay "all right" too, won't you?'

She could not answer: she did not know what to say.

'I must go to my performance now. I'll come and see you on Sunday afternoon, to make sure you are well. You will be in?'

'We should be delighted,' Rachel answered.

'*Arrivederci* then.'

'Goodbye.'

Rachel put the 'phone down. 'Giuseppe Marcello', she half sang to herself. 'What a lovely name.'

She wandered slowly back to Bridge House. It was only now that she noticed a most beautiful sunset, brilliant and delicate pink, floating across the sky, and promising sunshine the next day.

*　　　*　　　*

On the following day, the Fire Brigade pumped out the surplus water, and all the Davids worked with Miss Drube to restore order on the ground floor. Cousin Luke walked round with his stick, looking bewildered amongst all the activity. As they were about to retreat to their own flat, he astonished them by inviting them all to lunch on Sunday.

When the time came, Rachel suspected that Miss Drube enjoyed herself most, as she had prepared a huge meal, which the Davids ate with constraint, feeling strange looking out from the ground floor on to the familiar garden. Even Tatiana ate a modest amount.

Cousin Luke tried hard to be amiable. He told Matthias about his music box, and they looked at it together, discussing the mechanism. He asked Matthias about the street piano, and Mrs David about her opera recordings. Then he brought out old photographs for Mrs David, Rachel and Tatiana to see.

When it seemed polite to do so, they said thank you and were prepared to go back to their flat. In the hall, they hesitated.

'Please, use the main staircase,' Cousin Luke requested, and went back towards his own room.

As they crossed the hall Matthias murmured:

'A bit of a strain, but it might have been worse. A decent lunch too. I didn't know Miss Drube could cook.'

'He was quite nice,' Tatiana admitted.

'He was doing his best to be normal and friendly, and that is so much better that I could sing for relief,' Mrs David said, smiling warmly at Rachel.

'Send for Cherubino. She's better than you!' Matthias teased her.

'Rachel,' Cousin Luke was calling. 'Could you come back for one moment, please?'

'Please again!' Matthias raised his eyebrows. 'How the old man has changed.'

Rachel went downstairs. Cousin Luke led the way into the pink room. The History of Bridge House was back again

149

on the little table. He opened it and showed her a fresh page.

On it was written: 'A new chapter.'

'It was not Murdoch who convinced me, but you.'

'But I've done nothing. I'd like to do things.'

'You have been here, your feet firmly planted in the twentieth century, trying to grow healing herbs at Bridge House.'

'That was just gardening, and herbs because they're good for cooking.'

'And medicine. At least,' he smiled genuinely, 'good medicine for my generation. I suspect that future patients of yours will need few herbs or new-fangled drugs. They will receive another, better treatment and care. And,' he hurried on, as if almost shy of what he had said, 'one more thing to show you.'

He turned to the front page. Below the dedication to Amelia, he had written:

'And for Rachel, who will know the future of the House.'

'You mean you will let us stay here? We shall stay beyond the trial period?'

'As long as you wish. And I shall leave the book to you, to complete.'

'To continue,' Rachel corrected him, something she would not have dared to do only a few days ago.

'To continue,' he agreed. 'And this house will reflect you. Have you not observed how houses tend to reflect their owners?'

Rachel nodded, thinking of their first impression of a gaunt house and Cousin Luke, but all she said was: 'Thank you from all of us,' quietly. She saw him settle himself in the pink armchair, his stick beside him.

She ran up the back stairs to tell them the news, but Tatiana spoke first, bursting with excitement:

'Did you see the mirror?'

'No. What about it?'

'It's gone. Broken away. So it *is* the end of the spell. I wonder how it happened? The floods couldn't have reached that far, could they? So that proves it. *I* must have broken it. The spell is broken, once and for all,' she said dramatically, enjoying herself.

'Well, I'm not so sure about that,' Mrs David said, looking a little amused. 'Though if water had cracked anything it would have been the wooden frame, which is odd. And the water didn't rise beyond the first few stairs, certainly not as far as the landing, did it, Rachel?'

'No. I've just nipped up the back way to tell you all what he said.'

She gave them the news that Cousin Luke now seemed certain that he wanted them to stay.

'For once, it isn't Tatiana who's bewitched someone then. It's you who's got round the old man,' Matthias commented.

'No more spells from anyone, thank you,' Tatiana said. 'I'm glad his old mirror's gone. Not that I'd mind a big new one for practising,' she added unrepentantly.

Rachel was intrigued, and, as soon as she could, went away to look for herself.

The black curtain was drawn back. Only the gold frame hung on the wall, empty of glass. The wooden panel carrying the inscription had been taken away too. Tatiana's spell, as she called it, was broken. No one could now peer in the looking-glass.

Rachel felt sure that it was no accident. The mirror had deliberately been broken away from the frame which had held it and the reflections of the past. As she looked consideringly, she was no longer mystified. For she had seen on Cousin Luke's stick scratches and scrapes. In the night she had heard banging in the distance, but had blamed it on late traffic, or repairs to damaged property. Only that morning, Miss Drube had filled an old tea chest in the backyard with rubbish.

And Cousin Luke was a very tall man.